Deep D

G000167107

Deep Dish Pizza Disaster

Book 5 in The Cast Iron Skillet Mystery Series

Jodi Rath

Cover Design by Karen Phillips at Phillips Covers
www.PhillipsCovers.com

Edited by Rebecca Grubb at Sterling Words
www.sterlingwords.com

Formatted by Merry Bond at Anessa Books
http://anessabooks.com

Published by MYS ED LLC
PO Box 349, Carroll, OH 43112
jrath@columbus.rr.com
https://www.jodirath.com

Leavensport, Ohio

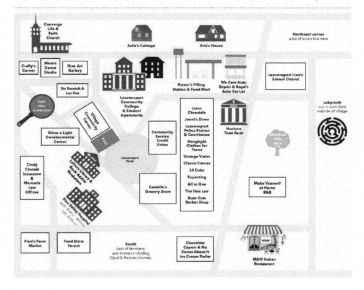

"I live inside books—I just exist outside of them." *~Taylor R. Williams*

Taylor is a supportive reader of the series and made this comment on my Author Jodi Rath Facebook page, and I asked permission to use it as a quote for this book!

Dedication

First off, I want to thank the readers. I know—it sounds cliché, but here's the thing: this is my second year as a cozy mystery writer. As of November of this year, I will have officially been a published cozy mystery writer for two full years, and in that time, I've written seven books in the series and currently finishing up the eighth as we speak. In that short, short amount of time, I've created an author page on Facebook where I've been fortunate enough to have approximately 5,000 likes—these men and women follow me, like my posts, comment, message, and email me regularly—daily for many. They are all incredibly kind, funny, and intelligent. Next, I started a Mystery-A-Month newsletter in November of 2018—zero subscribers when I started led to nearly 10,000 now. Again, so many subscribers were responding to my mystery every month that I had to join Rafflecopter and do them there because there weren't enough hours in the day to reply to each email the way I wish I could. You have to believe me when I tell you that NEVER in my WILDEST dreams would I EVER think I would have this kind of following! I'm getting close to 30,000 followers total on all social media, including the newsletter—what blows my mind EVEN more is that there have only been a handful of trolls in the bunch—*barely*! Everyone in the cozy-reading community is absolutely amazing and supportive. I tell my husband all the time that it freaks me out because I genuinely feel that I know all of you—like we've met and hung out. So, THANK YOU to each and every one of you that follows me somewhere and engages and interacts. You make my entire world complete!

Now, to focus on a few specific names! Leila Gaskill is a top fan that signs up for every one of my raffles and she follows me to all my social media takeovers. She sends me the SWEETEST messages and has sent me kind letters through snail mail! I'm in love with her sweet, beautiful spirit. She inspires me daily to be a better person! Next, Taylor R. Williams and I chat like old friends do on the phone, only instead, through comments on my posts! LOL! She is the one who came up with that AMAZING quote for this book—it just popped into her head, and she wrote it on my author Jodi Rath Facebook page. I asked if it was a famous quote, and Taylor said, "Nope, just came up with it!" So, of course, I pleaded with her, "PLWEASSSE let me use it in the next book!" Of course, she agreed—who can say no to an adult talking baby-talk? LOL!

While I've had my share of some in the industry who have been less than kind, I've been WAY more fortunate to make many WONDERFUL and professional friends in the writing industry! Two of my all-time favorites are Dakota Cassidy and Dionne Lister. They are my faves as writers and because I LOVE their cozy work—be sure to check out both authors if you are looking for more great cozies to read!

Next, one of the raffles I did this year asked for ideas for two new characters in this book—then I expanded on that in a Cozy Takeover on Facebook. Jamie Rutland Gillepsie came up with Baggy's character, and Crystal Lassiter-Zky came up with

Myrtle's character! Thanks, ladies! I hope I did your characters justice!

As always, thanks to Karen Phillips, Merry Bond and Rebecca Grubb, who help to perfect every book in this series.

Last but not least, my friends and family who put up with my INSANE schedule. I don't think any of them truly understand how much or how hard I work, but they grudgingly accept it! LOL! Now, my hubby and my nine cats understand how much and how hard I work and they all accept it graciously and support me no matter what—even in my absolute INSANE moments of pulling my wild curls out of my head when I'm not on track to meet a deadline or I can't figure out a scene or how the book should end or—or—or! You get it!

Sincerely,

The Leavensport Crew

Jolie Tucker—Co-owner of Cast Iron Creations, born in the village, best friend of Ava, granddaughter of Opal, daughter of Patty.

Ava Martinez—Co-owner of Cast Iron Creations, born in the village, best friend of Jolie, girlfriend of Delilah, sister of Lolly, daughter of Sophia and Thiago.

Keith—Ex-boyfriend of Jolie, born in the village, best friend of Teddy—now, an officer of Leavensport.

Detective Mick Meiser—Love interest of Jolie, from Tri-City, transferred career to Leavensport.

Chief Teddy Tobias—Police chief of Leavensport and born in the village, best friend of Keith.

Lydia—Jolie's frenemy, dating Bradley (or is she?) village nurse, best friend of Betsy, born in the village.

Betsy—Owns Chocolate Capers, best friend of Lydia, born in the village.

Delilah—Sister of Bradley, village artist, girlfriend of Ava.

Bradley—Brother of Delilah, village journalist.

Grandma Opal—Jolie's grandma, housewife who helped Jolie and Ava start Cast Iron Creations with her cast-iron skillet recipes.

Aunt Fern—Jolie's wacky, unpredictable aunt, sister to Patty, man-hungry.

Patty—Jolie's mom.

Mayor Nalini—mayor of Leavensport, Lahiri is his niece.

Jackson Nestle—Unscrupulous political associate of Mayor Cardinal from Tri-City

Tink—Jolie's cousin that she only recently realized she had.

Tom Costello—grocer in Leavensport; dating Grandma Opal

Eddie—uncle to Jolie. Was estranged from family for decades with wife Shelly and five kids.

Wylie—uncle to Jolie.

Ralph—owns Ralph's pizza in Tri-City

Stella—works with Peggy and Ralph in Tri-City

Mayor Cardinal—mayor of Tri-City

Tonya Morrison—assistant to Mayor Cardinal

Elijah Morrison—Tonya's son who is in college.

Zed and Zander Zimmerman—brothers who are farmers in Leavensport.

Miles Milano—brother to Detective Mick Meiser/Milano.

Marty Milano—brother to Detective Mick Meiser/Milano.

Maya Milano—Mick's mother.

Maddox Milano—Mick's father.

Dr. Delagada—Meisers' neurologist

Zacharia—Leavensport handyman

Jason—Teddy's brother

Chuck—Jolie's biological father.

Prologue

Lydia's screams alarmed everyone at the Leavensport Labor Day festival. All eyes were on her as she began going into labor. Her water had broken, and she was bent over in pain, screaming profanities that would make even Ava blush. I saw Mick had rushed over to her, coaching her to breathe while the makeshift ambulance–two paramedics in a golf cart–zipped through the crowd toward her. The siren stuck to the top of the golf cart wailed, alerting festival-goers to move out of the way, but it did not drown out Lydia's shrieks of pain.

Being sensitive to noises, I began to pace and look around in a panic when I noticed Ralph, from Ralph's Pizza Shop in Tri-City, standing behind his booth. He was frozen, staring off into space, and didn't seem to notice the commotion around Lydia, which was bewildering. I watched him as the chaos continued all around me. His eyes bulged as he stumbled against the corner of his booth, grasping at the cloth, then falling to one knee. He grabbed his throat. Was he choking? I ran around the booth to his side...

Chapter One

Saturday, September 19, 2020

"He was dead. No one could find any wounds on his body. Meanwhile, she was having the baby at the same time at the festival—you already know all of this!" I raised my voice as I sat across from the brown eyes I knew so well. The ones I grew to love over the last two years.

August 29, 2020

Those hot, stale summer months had turned into breezy, brisk autumn days. Our little village of Leavensport's annual Lively Lavish Labor Day Festival was coming up next weekend, and I was working hard to prepare a cast iron feast to sell at Cast Iron Creations' booth. The festival brought in all of the locals, as well as many Tri-City merchants setting up booths to promote their businesses. Every year it seemed more and more people from around Ohio made the trip to our little village to enjoy the festivities. It did wonders to stimulate our local economy.

This would be the first year I'd run the booth with Ava and my official boyfriend, Detective Mick Meiser. Mick and I had now been together for nearly four months, and I'd never been happier. My grandma was engaged to Tom Costello, Leavensport grocer, Ava had plans to propose to

Delilah soon, and Aunt Fern and Mayor Nalini were still dating. Love was definitely in the air in Leavensport!

"Hey, can you spare a minute to help me up front? Magda had to run a quick errand, and we just got a rush," Ava stuck her head back through the push-through kitchen doors.

"Sure thing, let me *pop* these cast iron *pop*overs in the oven, and I'll *pop* right out." I waggled my eyebrows at her and grinned.

"LAME." Ava rolled her large chestnut brown eyes, but I saw the start of a smile form as she turned back to the dining area.

I strolled out front and my blue eyes widened at the packed tables before me, "What's going on? This is an odd time for a rush like this. I don't recognize a lot of these as regulars."

"Tri-City folk coming in to begin getting their booths set up for next weekend. I'd imagine Meiser's place is hopping, too. Chocolate Capers will probably get a lot of business later before they head back to the city," Ava said.

"Good point. I'll text Betsy and give her a heads up." I grabbed my phone and sent off a quick text to our friend, then grabbed an ordering pad and pen in one hand and coffee pot in the other and began moving around to get some orders going and cups filled.

Lydia waddled in with Magda following close behind her. "Whoa, sorry, I never would have run out if I would have known we would get slammed!" Magda grabbed the coffee pot and the pad from me and took over.

"Hey, Jolie." Lydia rubbed her pregnant belly and blew out a long breath.

"You need to sit down at the counter for a minute?" I asked. Lydia and I had a lifetime of being frenemies. The last few months is the longest that we have been consistently pleasant to one another.

"If I can fit," she laughed.

"You're due soon, yes?" I asked, filling up a cup of hot water and giving her a small cast-iron box with a variety of tea flavors.

"Thanks, yeah, I'm past due. I'm so ready to have this child." She poked around for something decaffeinated.

"Hey, Ava, can you grab Lydia what she needs, please? I need to get back to the kitchen to check on the popovers and start working on all these orders," I said, smiling and waving to Lydia.

Time flew by as I scrambled to get to all the orders. I had just finished sending out the last of the rush when Carlos, our assistant manager and other cook came in for the dinner shift.

"Yabba dabba doo, Jolie, you should have called me. I would have come in early to help you," Carlos said, pointing to his Flintstone's T-shirt. He learned English from American cartoons and loved to wear character shirts every day.

"We didn't expect to get hit so hard. It just happened, and I just kept cooking," I said, wiping sweat from my brow, then walking to the sink to splash some water on my face and wash my hands.

"Well, I'm here now to take over." Carlos began cleaning up.

"I can clean up, and I'm so sorry I didn't get more prep done for you for tonight. I started on the poblano-stuffed peppers—there are a few trays of them in the fridge." I pointed to our huge stainless steel refrigerator.

"That's great! And it looks like it has started to clear out there. I should be fine. You go and relax." Carlos smiled at me.

I decided to take him up on that. I grabbed my large brown leather tote from the office and moved up front to see if Ava was ready to head home. We always walked, biked, or drove—depending on the weather—to work together. Today was a beautiful sunny day, but we needed to stop by Fred the Farmer's Market to pick up some local fruits and veggies for some dishes I was preparing for next weekend. I liked to make things first to sample before the real-deal event.

"All set?" I asked her, grabbing my keys.

Mirabelle, our hostess with the mostess, had just been dropped off by her mom, Mary, and she had Spy, her seeing-eye dog with her up front. Mirabelle was in her twenties, short, pleasantly plump, with the hugest and most beautiful smile and a great personality. Everyone adored her, and when it wasn't her shift to work, people always asked where she was.

"Hey, girlfriend!" Ava said, walking toward the exit. She and Mirabelle did their fist bump explosion, and Spy wiggled his tush as he sat near his best buddy.

"Hi, Ava!" Mirabelle squealed in glee.

"Hey, what am I? Chopped liver?" I asked, palms up.

Mirabelle giggled, "Hi, Jolie!"

Spy gave a quiet woof.

"Hi, sweet lady," I said, hugging her. "You know, everyone has been asking where you were today. We tell them you can't work open to close every day. You are one popular woman!"

Mirabelle's smile spread across her face. "Really?"

"Of course, everyone loves you WAY better than they do Jolie," Ava said.

I froze and glared at Ava. Mirabelle laughed. I walked out the door, shaking my head all the way to my car.

Driving to the farmers market, I decided to take the long way and drive past the Village Community Center, Leisure Library, and Book Addict Bookstore since I loved to see the displays they all did around festival time to promote their businesses. The library had large inflatable dancing men and women dressed as different workers for Labor Day weekend. I checked my rearview mirror and not seeing anyone behind me, then I slowed to a crawl to carefully look at the display window of books.

"Why don't you just pull over and park, and we can go in?" Ava asked.

"Oh, okay!" I said, pulling off to the side to parallel park. I was the worst at this, and it was part of the reason I didn't want to pull over. The streets were lined with cars because of the festival. I pulled up, put my arm around Ava's seat, and began to slowly back in, but I cut too sharp. I pulled back out to the street and set up again.

"Do you want to get out, and I'll do it?" Ava suppressed a giggle.

"I got it," I simultaneously shook my head and rolled my eyes, hoping to get it right this time.

I took my position, this time not turning the wheel too sharply, and backed in slowly, then stopped.

"Why are you stopping? Pull back a bit more, then straighten out the wheel," Ava said.

"Just be quiet! You're making me nervous! This is a tight squeeze, Ava." I noticed she blew out a breath and looked out the window, knowing watching me would freak me out more.

"Hey, Miss Tucker, be careful, you're going to hit that car!"

I braked hard and saw Jason Tobias, Teddy's teen brother, standing rigid with hands out, pleading me to stop.

"Here, let me do it, I've been practicing." Jason darted around the car and reached for my keys with gleaming eyes.

"Um ..." I hesitated.

"We're never going to get out if you don't let him," Ava said.

I put the car in park and got out to let Jason in, and then I watched as Jason smoothly pulled out to start over, carefully eased the car in at an angle, and then straightened it out, perfectly centering the car between the blue sedan in front and the red truck behind me.

Jason popped out, gave me a huge grin and handed my keys back, and then darted across the street when he saw one of his buddies from high school who I heard yell, "Man, you nailed that parking! No doubt, you are passing your driver's test!"

Ava burst out laughing, bending over at the waist. I felt my face turn five shades of red. "Don't say a word!" I pointed in her face as I walked past her.

Ava, who now had a few tears forming from laughing so hard at a sixteen-year-old showing me up on parallel parking, gave me the scout's honor finger sign, and we began walking toward the bookstore and library displays. The library had a lot of non-fiction books on the origin and spirit of Labor Day, while the bookstore's display offered Labor Day-themed fictional books with vintage canvas bunting American flags hanging behind the books.

"Are we going in?" Ava asked.

"No, just looking," I said as I saw my Aunt Fern and Grandma Opal approaching us from the community center. "Oh, crap! This is exactly why I didn't want to stop!" I snapped at Ava.

"Don't blame me because your family is nuts!" Ava snapped back.

"Yoo-hoo! Ladies—" my Aunt Fern waved us down as I tried to steer Ava toward the car.

"They see us! Stop pushing me—plus, you know you can't get out of that parking spot that quickly anyway!" Ava yelled.

"Girls, stop!" Grandma Opal yelled in a curt voice.

We froze.

"Oh, hey, didn't see you there. We need to head over to Fred the Farmer's Farm Market to pick up a few things," I said, smiling and waving as I led Ava, who was trying to turn and wave while being drug by her elbow to the car.

"Jolie Lynn Tucker!" Grandma exclaimed. "Who taught you those manners?"

"You, mom, Aunt Fern, and Uncle Wylie," I said, giving up and crossing my arms across my chest.

Grandma's eyes narrowed, and she shook her head.

"Whoa, Aunt Fern, is that a new necklace to match your earrings?" Ava reached out to touch the gold necklace.

"Yep, Fitan got it for me."

I still wasn't used to hearing anyone call the mayor by his first name, and it freaked me out a bit. Mayor Nalini had courted my Aunt Fern as her secret admirer at the beginning of the summer. That was when Ava and I tried our hand at online cooking courses that turned out to be disastrous in more ways than one. One of our students, Lahiri, who had been a co-conspirator, was now free as a bird, and we found out she is related to Fitan Nalini. I still wondered if that is why she got off so easily—it still wasn't sitting well with me. I tried talking to Aunt Fern about it before, but she would have *no trash talk about her man.* I vowed to Aunt Fern, after a lot of strong-arming on her part, to attempt to behave decently toward Lahiri. Truth be told, I planned to avoid her at all costs, and behave as best I could when forced to interact with her.

"Very nice," I said. "Were you two working at the community center?"

"Yeah, we were setting up the dining room and helping to get things set up in the kitchen as much as possible. We want people to have the opportunity to eat and socialize inside if they so choose this weekend," Grandma said.

"There's still a whole week ahead. There's no events or meetings this coming week?" I asked.

"Nope, Fitan put everything off so we could get a head start to make this year's festival the best ever!" Behind those large, thick-rimmed glasses, Aunt Fern had a look of love in her eyes.

"What decorations are you using?" Ava asked.

By the look on both of their faces, that seemed to be a sore topic.

"You know they have that stupid pole on the stage for some reason—" Grandma started.

"It's a beam to help keep the roof from falling in," Aunt Fern declared.

"Whatever. It looks like a stripper pole to me."

Ava and I side-eyed each other nervously.

"Anyhoo, I thought it would be a kick to get a male blow-up doll and make him into a Magic Mike character for the stage. You know, put him on the pole." Grandma put her hands on her hips.

I stood frozen in my spot while my indigo eyes darted around inside my sockets. I could see Ava's body trembling, probably to contain a laugh.

"Right? Isn't that the most cockeyed idea you girls have ever heard in your life?" Aunt Fern shook her head as loose curls bobbed around her face. "I'm going to need to go see that therapist of yours with a mother trying to recreate strip scenes from movies!"

"I'm not touching that with a ten-foot pole," I said as Ava could no longer hold it in and barked out a hearty laugh. The two of us ran and jumped into my car and sped off toward the farmers market.

"Seriously," I started as we pulled into the parking lot, "what is wrong with them?"

"Come on, they're funny!"

"Sometimes, I'll admit to finding them a tad humorous, but man, can they ever give me a headache."

"Yeah, you did NOT get your sense of humor from them," Ava said as we moved toward the outside part of the market.

"You're not funny either," I said.

Ava pushed my shoulder, shoving me into the driver's side window. We grew up together, and I was an only child, but Ava had a sister, Lolly. Ava and I were like siblings and best friends all in one. Our relationship was difficult for those who did not know us from birth to understand. There was a lot of loving bantering between us.

Fred the farmer stood outside under his red-and-white-striped awning, near the bales of hay with pumpkins of every size scattered around. Vibrant red, orange, yellow, and purple mums were displayed everywhere with boxes filled with pale yellow squashes and green zucchini and the like. Large bins of fresh-picked red and green apples were displayed on tables and nestled up next to them were large bowls of grapes and pears and buckets of cranberries.

"Well, if it isn't the two best-lookin' ladies in the village! Why am I the luckiest farmer ever to have you two grace me with your presence?" Fred stood, beaming a broad smile. He was a favorite of most people in the town, including me. Fred Edie stood about five-foot-five and always wore some sort of overalls or coveralls and work boots or rubber boots to match the weather and task. Today he sported his bibs with a green t-shirt underneath and brown leather work boots. His graying hair was full and parted to the side, and his square-jawed face had the well-earned wrinkles typical of a man who had worn a smile most of his life while working out in the sun.

"Hi, Mr. Fred the Farmer." Ava grinned. This is what she had called him since she was a kid.

"Hey, Fred! Your produce looks amazing as always!"

"You own this place?" asked a tall, lanky man with thick, black hair, a long narrow chin, and a mole under his nose.

"Sure do, sir, what can I do for you today?"

"I'm Ralph and own the pizza shop in Tri-City. I've heard great things about your produce. I figured while I was setting up my booth, I'd come here and buy the veggies for my pizzas for this week before the festival starts." Ralph enunciated each syllable of each word, making his sentences choppy, and his tone seem demanding even though he seemed friendly enough by appearance.

"Whoa!" I exclaimed. "I'm Jolie Tucker, and this is my friend Ava—we run Cast Iron Creations. We've had your New York-style pizza, and I have to tell you, it's incredible. Out of this world!"

"Well, thanks for the compliment, dear. I'll pass it right back atcha. I just came from your shop for a bit of lunch. That skillet-fried chicken with cast-iron skillet-wilted bok choy seemed like an odd combo to me, but man, it packed a punch!"

"Thanks! I'm not a pizza genius like you, but I love to make deep-dish pizzas in cast iron."

"Oh, yeah? Maybe I'll try that next weekend as another option inspired by you," Ralph said, nodding his head as he moved toward the zucchini.

"Hey, beautiful." I heard Mick's voice behind me and felt tingles go up and down my spine. I turned toward him, smiling. I spun around and froze with worry as I saw him sitting in a wheelchair.

Chapter Two

That night, Mick and I sat on my back deck overlooking the apple trees, flower garden filled with the mums that had grown in, and my vegetable and herb garden that wouldn't last much longer.

"Why didn't you tell me all of this before?" My mind was racing as fast as my heart. I was terrified of what all this meant for our future.

Mick sat, staring at his hands awkwardly before saying, "I'm sorry. I told you before, I can't control what happens with this MS or when it happens. That's why I did that trial last winter. I started noticing worse balance issues, then weakness in my legs after being on my feet too long."

"You told me all that, but what you didn't tell me is that this was a possibility." That felt harsh to say to him, but I felt like he owed me an explanation. We are supposed to be in everything together.

"I guess I didn't want to think this was a possibility, Jolie. And why would I want to share it with the woman I'm in love with?"

We'd vaguely declared our love for each other in the past, but this was the first time Mick had directly told me he was in love with me. I felt tears well up in my baby blues and reached out for his hand. "Babe, listen, whatever happens in our life, we are in it together. I told you before that I'm all in, and I mean that. I love you so much."

Squeezing my hand, Mick pulled me to him, and we embraced.

"I have an appointment with my neurologist tomorrow morning. You've never been with me to meet her. Why don't you come with me so you can ask any questions you have?"

"Yeah, I really want to be there. So, you aren't in a wheelchair for good, but you could be. Is that right?"

"Right now, that's true. We need to talk to her about this tomorrow."

I nodded my head as we headed to bed, where I knew I wouldn't be able to sleep, wondering what all I'd learn tomorrow. "Uh—oh, are you—"

"I've been sleeping on my couch and not going upstairs at home right now," Mick looked down at his legs. "I can go home tonight."

"Nope, bet you didn't know this is a pullout, did you?" I grinned, shoving the coffee table out of the way and turning the couch into a bed.

I pushed Mick into the Pine Valley Hospital. Our village population was so small that all the doctors, dentists, and eye doctors were housed on the ground floor of the hospital. Mick's MS doctor was on the sixth floor with the other specialists, so we took the elevator up. Even though it was a smaller hospital, the building had modern architecture with a large, arched, revolving glass entrance, brick, and shiny silver overhanging and trim along the building. It had comfy seating in the lobby, a cafeteria to the left for staff and visitors—every so often, we brought some cast iron dishes for the staff to sell.

As we were waiting in the elevator, Meiser grumbled, "Normally, I would take the stairs to help stay in shape."

Standing behind the wheelchair, I pretended not to hear him. I had no idea how to respond. I needed to know more from his doctor. I was trying so hard to act right—but I didn't know what that meant. I didn't want to be overly bubbly, but I was avoiding being negative or babying him. I was surprised he let me push the wheelchair from the parking lot inside. He seemed deflated, and I couldn't tell if it was physical or if he was bothered by me being here learning all about his MS.

Meiser took over, pushing himself into the doctor's office lobby and went to the window to check-in. I sat and began reading a copy of *Southern Cast Iron* magazine that was on the table.

"What are you reading?" Meiser wheeled up to me.

"Lots of great apple-picking cast iron recipes." I held up the magazine, and all of the subscription inserts fluttered to the floor.

I slapped my forehead, exasperated at my clumsiness, then walked around the wheelchair to where one lay in the middle of the floor. I bent and knocked my head into something soft and bouncy.

I looked up to see Lydia's pregnant belly. "Oh, I'm so sorry, are you okay?"

"Yeah," she said, rubbing her bump. "I'd have offered to pick them up, but who knows if I'd ever stand up straight again."

"Is it time for another baby check-up?"

Lydia's eyes darted from Mick to me in panic. My stomach turned.

"She's here to be with me," Mick said.

"I didn't know you'd be here too," Lydia stammered.

I looked back and forth from Mick to Lydia, unconsciously rubbing my sweaty palms on my jeans—my nervous tick.

"I told you when you were in Santo Domingo that Lydia came to appointments with me. She's helped me make some plans on how to handle all this."

"Right, you did tell me that," I said tersely.

"Mick," a nurse popped her head out a door and looked around the waiting room. "We need to do your tests."

"I'm going to head out," Lydia said, turning toward the exit.

"I'm sorry, this is my fault, I forgot to call and let you know Jolie was coming with me today."

"Not an issue, you know what I'll do." She smiled at Mick.

"Getting a hot fudge sundae for the baby, right?" Mick laughed.

She nodded at him as I felt a fake smile spread across my face. I waved at Lydia and moved to wheel Mick in, but he grabbed the handles and did it himself.

We moved into the office, and I sat in a corner thinking about one of my favorite older movies, *Dirty Dancing*, and how I was so unlike Baby—everyone puts this baby in a corner.

"Sorry, I know that was uncomfortable," Mick said.

"Yeah, I—"

"Mick," the nurse called again.

"Sorry, I'll go do this really quickly if you want to wait. The doctor won't be there. It is just some physical tests they make me do—vision, walking, coordination and a quick blood test." He looked uncomfortably at me. "I would kind of rather do this part by myself."

I was still reeling from Lydia's appearance, so I just nodded. He disappeared through the door with the nurse and I stared, unseeing, at the magazine. *He and Lydia act like best friends. Or more! But she was there for him when things got rough. And I trust him. I think? I'm bad at trusting people.*

I'm not sure how many minutes went by before the door swung open and the nurse looked right at me. "Jolie, right?" I nodded. "He finished his checks and now he's in an exam room. He asked me to come get you."

I followed her past the receptionist's desk and down a hallway, into a room. Mick was sitting in his wheelchair. He looked up and smiled. "Dr. Delagada will be in in just a second," said the nurse as she left.

"Sorry—" Mick began again, but almost immediately, the door opened again.

A short, muscular woman with brown hair that was in a bob came speed walking into the exam room.

"Hello, Mr. Meiser. Nice to see you again," she said. Her words moved as briskly as her legs.

"Hi, Dr. Delagada, this is my girlfriend, Jolie Tucker," Meiser introduced me.

"Hi, it's nice to—"

Dr. Delagada quickly shook my hand, one quick, curt shake, then opened Mick's file, cutting me off. "I see you need a wheelchair now. You are still walking and only using as needed, correct?" She kept her head still in the folder but glanced up at Mick.

"Yeah, I've found it's easier to use the wheelchair more, though."

"Not what I want to hear. If you don't need it, then don't use it. You don't want to get used to it," Dr. Delagada stated bluntly.

"I think he's a little depressed. I'm not sure he saw all of this—"

"Yes, that makes sense. I can prescribe something for the emotions, but you need to use your legs as much as possible. Keep the wheelchair with you at all times in case you need it—but I'd rather see you walking on your own or with a cane or a walker before the wheelchair."

Again, lightning-speed talking. Between the Lydia encounter and this woman's behavior, I was about ready to lose it. I took a deep breath in and saw Meiser glance nervously at me.

"Dr. Delagada, I'm here today because I haven't been in the loop. I want to know what is going on, and I feel like I'm getting only part of the story. I was out of town for a month in the winter when he started having more balance issues. So, you are saying there is no need for the wheelchair?" I felt my voice was diplomatic enough for how grated my nerves felt in the moment.

Dr. Delagada looked to Meiser, "Why haven't you shared what all you've dealt with to date? Do you not want her to know?"

Wow, another deep breath—I'm assuming she is referring to doctor-patient confidentiality.

"She's who I have listed to contact in case of emergency, and I've signed all the forms so that she can know everything," Mick said.

Without thinking, I blurted out, "You never told me that!"

"It seems we need to all be on the same page," Dr. Delagada said as she flipped to the beginning of Mick's chart.

"Sorry, it's not something I enjoy talking about."

"Well, it seems like you need to get used to talking about it. I'm going to recommend that you start taking Lexipro. Depression is normal for anyone that has an autoimmune disease. I think it would be best to seek counseling as well. I think a combination of talking to someone, the Lexipro, and you relying on your legs again will help you feel more in control and help you address your feelings in a productive way."

"I agree." I shifted in my seat, crossing my legs and arms at the same time.

"Okay, let's start at the beginning. Stop me if you have questions." Dr. Delagada looked up at me. "Mr. Meiser presented symptoms of balance issues, and it was first diagnosed as vertigo, but he didn't recover. This happened several years ago, and the MS went undiagnosed for a little over a year."

"Is that normal?" I asked, astounded. "How could someone think vertigo when it's something so much more serious than that—and for *that* long?"

"He went to a general doctor who would assume it is something like vertigo. You have to understand there is not an official diagnosis for MS.

Generally, a full neurological work-up is needed, and even then, it comes down to ruling things out before we realize it is MS."

"That's why I didn't tell you. It wasn't to keep anything from you. There's a lot to it. It's confusing to me, so I'm not sure how to explain it to someone else."

"Not to mention, I haven't always been the easiest person for you to talk to," I said, averting my eyes from his gaze.

Dr. Delagada briefly scanned the chart. "Once diagnosed, he started on a daily dose of Gilyena, which he took for quite some time. It's not uncommon for an MS patient to have to switch their meds regularly.Research for a cure is happening all the time, so trial treatments and medications come out from time to time as well."

"I knew you were taking that medicine," I said. "I saw it in your cabinet in the bathroom at your house."

"It stopped having an effect, so we put him in a trial, which didn't work. Because it didn't work, it caused RRMS—Relapsing-Remitting MS, which is why he is struggling with weakness of his legs right now."

"So, what now?" I asked.

"Your blood test came back negative for JC, so you are safe to start Tysabri. It's a drug that has proven to help many improve their strength. It's important you understand what I am about to tell you," the doctor said.

"Hold on," I said, reaching into my tote bag to grab the little journal I kept in there and a pen. "Okay, go ahead. Er—hold on." I wrote "RRMS" down.

"Okay, first off, he has had what's called a relapse. This means that he took a few steps back on his progress. He won't return to one hundred percent again. He will improve, but he will hit a new normal. So, you need to expect that you will have times when you will have more weakness than other times. This is why I am telling you to not depend on the wheelchair, cane, or walker *if* you don't need to do so." Dr. Delagada gave a hard stare at Meiser who looked away defiantly.

"I'll make sure he doesn't." I scribbled a note.

I felt Mick glaring into my soul.

"You are going to find you have other issues down the road, and there is no rhyme or reason to it. Also, the new medicine, Tysabri, is a once a month infusion you will take. It may work wonders, or it may do nothing. Time will tell."

"How soon will we know if it works?" Mick asked.

"Like everything else with this disease, it's impossible to know. I can tell you that most people will see a difference pretty quickly. It could look different for you, though."

"Great." His face was void of expression.

"We'll deal with whatever comes our way," I said, noting what she just said.

"I want him to get going on therapy and the Lexipro and set up the first infusion for after labor day. Then I want to see him three months after the infusion. At six months, we'll do an MRI and look at the lesions. At some point, we will discuss PML. I don't want to do it now. He is JC negative currently, so there is no need."

"What is that?" I asked.

"You don't want to know," Meiser said.

I felt my stomach sink.

"I'll talk to you about it later. I know what it is. I have some pamphlets, and I've talked to Lydia about it," Mick said.

Dr. Delagada wrote out some scripts and spoke to a nurse about setting some things up, then looked up at us. "Any more questions before I leave?"

"No—" "Yes," Meiser and I said at the same time.

"Sorry, the RRMS you mentioned is that only for the weakness in legs?" I asked.

"Good question. No, it can be that, balance, driving, episodes that present like seizures for some, blindness at times—there are numerous things."

I wished I hadn't asked.

She must have seen that by the look on my face because she said, "Listen, this is a lot. But you can only deal with what is in front of you at the moment. Right now, all-in-all, you are doing very well. You need to get hold of this more productively mentally, which we are working on, and we will switch to Tysabri and take it from there. In the meantime, try to stand up and push that chair out and don't use it unless you absolutely have to— unless you want to be in a wheelchair for life."

With that, she speed-walked toward the nurses' station, said a few words, handed off Mick's folder, grabbed another, and speed-walked into a new room.

"You heard the woman. UP!" I said, getting up and swinging my large tote around my neck, crossover style.

Mick looked up at me, annoyed, and slowly pushed himself out of the wheelchair. I watched his legs shake a bit as he stood. When I saw he was watching me, I looked away quickly.

"You push the chair out to the van," I said, thinking it could help balance him and realizing I needed to stop babying him so much.

We had borrowed my Aunt Fern's new orange minivan, so we had room to put the wheelchair in the back. When we got to it, I went up front to the passenger side and threw my tote in it.

"What are you doing?" Mick asked.

"What? She said you can drive. You just walked out here."

"I don't think that's a good idea."

"Try it. If you struggle, pull over and I'll drive. What better way to find out?" I walked back, folded the wheelchair, and asked him to help me lift it in the back. I didn't need him to help, but I figured he needed to feel useful.

I held the keys out to him, and he hesitated. I jingled them impatiently.

"Okay, but if I get us in a wreck, you're the one dealing with your family, not me!"

"Deal!" I smiled to myself, feeling more like we were back in a groove.

Mick drove to M&M's, his Italian restaurant, to check in and see how everything was going.

"So, you said something about how this would have to be your main job now, but that's not really true after what Dr. Delagada just said, right?" I asked. It was hard to imagine Mick not being a detective.

"I don't know. I need to figure some things out."

"You are getting therapy, though, right? And you are filling that prescription?"

"Jolie, I need some time to think it all through before I medicate and go to therapy."

"It sounds like that will help you think it through."

He stopped and slammed his hands on the steering wheel. "Look, just back off for now, okay? This is all a lot to take in—" He looked at me and took a deep breath when he saw I was shocked by his level of anger. I felt my body deflate and went inside myself, looking out the window with a vacant stare.

"I'm sorry. I need to go in here and do a few things. Call Ava and have her get you. I'll have Mrs. Seevers follow me home and take the van to your Aunt Fern's since they are neighbors. Then I'll do a little thinking and get back to you." He reached over and kissed me quickly on the cheek, then got out. He dug through his bag and pulled out a foldable cane. He snapped it open and leaned on it as he walked carefully into the restaurant.

But he left the wheelchair in the van. That was progress.

I walked to the patio that overlooked the beautiful fields and woods that were up for sale and sat down and called Ava and asked if she could run over to get me.

"So, how'd it go?" Ava held the steering wheel tightly while looking straight ahead as we drove toward Cast Iron Creations.

"Weeeell—" "That good, huh?"

"It wasn't horrible, so there's that. Lydia was there."

"HUH?" Ava's eye bulged at me.

"Watch the road!" I yelled.

"Why?"

"I guess they got close—I mean, I knew they got closer when we were in the Dominican Republic—I thought they were an item—"

"You are doing that circling the toilet with your words again," Ava reminded me, knowing I tended to ramble when I was confused or afraid or upset.

"I'm trying to be strong for him while dealing with the shock of this. I totally mean it when I tell him I'm all in—no matter what. It's just a lot right now. I feel like a real jerk that Lydia showing up made me jealous. I mean, we're together—why am I jealous? Why is *that* at the forefront of my mind with everything else?"

"Because of your history with her. She's never given you a good reason to trust her. Then you've had so many people screw you over that you don't know who to trust," Ava said, bracing her arm against my seat and turning her head to parallel park in front of Sir Scratch A Lot, the vet across the street from our restaurant. Unlike me, she was smooth as a baby's bottom when it came to parallel parking.

We sat in the car for a moment before I spoke. "You're theraperizing me."

"Is that a word?"

"Just made it up."

"Well, you've done therapy and journal therapy for so long now and shared so much with me, I feel like I could fill in for Tabitha on some sessions—you know, like you could probably ace that PI exam and get your license in no time."

"I told you I can't take that on right now." I crossed my arms. Boundaries. I continually have to remind myself to keep to my limits.

"I know, but one day soon you'll do it. So, he can still walk, right?"

"Yeah," I proceeded to go through a lot, not all, of what the doctor said. Mick knew Ava and I told each other everything, but there were a few things I felt more comfortable letting him decide to tell people.

"Can you two still—" Ava bit her lower lip and looked away.

"What? Can we still have—"

"Yeah, I mean—"

"Well, I'm not sure how all that will work. I suspect I can take more control of the situation if I—"

"Stop! Enough!" Ava put her hands over her ears and closed her eyes. Why she closed her eyes, I had no clue.

"You asked me!" I squealed.

"I was looking for a simple yes or no! I didn't expect you to give me all the dirty deets on it!"

"Oh my gosh, let's just go in!"

Walking into our restaurant never got old to me. Delilah, Ava's girlfriend, transformed the entire wall to the right into a huge mural of our town. Big bay windows opened in the front, which were enhanced by the recent installation of a comfy counter bench with dark-chocolate-colored wood trim edged along the wall below with large tiles that turned into pullout drawers. Fluffy pillows that matched the colors in the restaurant were scattered around the bench. We worked with the local library, bookstore, and some of the women in the village to get a bunch of used books and magazines to store inside the bench and Zacharia, Leavensport's handy-man who could build or fix anything, had added some shelving to the side. Anyone could pick out a book or magazine, get cozy with some tea, coffee, or cocoa, and read by the window.

Ava pointed for me to sit there since no one else seemed to be occupying the space while she went to grab herself some coffee and held up a teabag from across the dining room. I shook my head no, pointed to the kitchen, did a charade of pouring something into a glass, and pumping something into the glass as Ava nodded in understanding.

"That's pretty impressive. It's a good thing I know you and Mick are a hot and heavy item, or I'd be jealous at how well my woman knows you," Delilah said, walking in and bending over to hug me. Her long, wavy hair flew into my face, and I caught a whiff of lavender.

"Yeah, it's a blessing and a curse to have a bestie who knows you so well," I said, slapping the cushion next to me for her to take a seat.

"What's a blessing and a curse?" Ava asked, walking up with her coffee and handing me my cold mocha drink, which I immediately sipped, then closed my eyes and moaned.

"Perfect ratio of two pumps of peppermint and some extra Hershey chocolate syrup," I said.

"That's what is a blessing and a curse," Delilah simply stated. "How well you know each other. I saw Jolie's little pantomime and thought it was cute how you knew exactly what she wanted."

"That's because that chica is extremely Type A-routine freakazoid—what would shock me is if she ever changed it up."

"You're dumb," I said, taking a few gulps of my caffeinated heavenly chocolate drink.

Delilah looked at Ava skeptically, and I knew she was questioning my lack of a creative, sassy comeback.

"She's having an off day. Probably why she needs the jolt of caffeine," Ava said, waving at Magda to bring Delilah some iced tea.

"See, she knows what you want too!" I said.

"I guess we are both easy to please. What's up to have you off your Ava game?" Delilah asked as Ava grimaced in our direction.

"A bunch of stuff with Mick. We'll work through it all, though. It's a lot to go into." I sipped my last few drinks slowly.

"Hey, I heard Lahiri is living with Mayor Nalini permanently now. I guess the two of them had an argument in front of your Aunt Fern and some others in the art district about him being too strict with her curfew. Then she accused him of taking the money she kept in her drawer for clubbing."

"Wow, maybe you should be on the case," I giggled at Ava.

"What's that supposed to mean?" Ava asked as Magda brought Delilah's iced tea with an orange peel in it like she liked.

"I mean, so far you've taken on the case of the missing cupcakes at Betsy's, Jayjay's lost dog that was at his big sister Dr. Libby, the vet's, the entire time, and little Willy Weatherton's missing fire truck. So, why not take on Lahiri's stolen club money?"

"You know what? Just because Mick is feeling sorry for himself and things are up in the air with his health, that doesn't give you a right to rain on my parade."

I bit my bottom lip and noticed Delilah looked concerned. "You're right, sorry."

"Speaking of that," Delilah changed the subject, "will they have the ramps installed at your houses and Mick's by the time he gets home?"

My jaw hung open. I completely forgot I asked Zacharia if he and his crew could add a ramp to Mick's side door where the step was, and on mine as well. Oh man, I totally jumped the gun on this one!

Chapter Three

I sat with a family-sized Hershey bar, gnawing through half of it after hearing that Zacharia and his crew had already installed the ramp at Mick's, but I caught them before they did anything at my house. He said he could remove it just as quickly, but not until tomorrow. That meant I had to wait for Mick to get home, find it, and then see how upset he would be with me.

I was down to the last two bites of my chocolate bar when my phone rang. I sat and stared at it, wondering if I should let it go to voicemail to hear what he had to say to prepare myself, but my stomach betrayed me with rumbles of sickness from all the sweets combined with stress, so I answered.

"Hello," I said innocently.

"There's a ramp here," Meiser snapped.

Okay, it seemed we weren't going to beat around the bush.

"Listen, I—"

Meiser interrupted me. "There is a ramp to my door. Someone came to my house in front of all my neighbors and put a ramp to my door, Jolie. It *screams* YOU!"

"Wow, now you are personifying the ramp," I chuckled hesitantly, trying to lighten the situation.

"No, this isn't cute. This isn't funny. You did this before you knew all the details. How irresponsible can you be?"

"Hold on a minute, Mick. I didn't know anything because you chose not to fill me in on anything. You did, however, tell Lydia everything. She's been going with you since—I don't even know how long!"

"So, your insensitivity is Lydia's fault now? Funny, I'm positive Lydia would never think to have a ramp put in without talking to me first."

"Hey—"

He hung up. Great. Just perfect.

After Mick hung up on me, I called Ava to come over for comfort and so she'd make me feel better about the situation. Not long after, I heard my doorknob turn.

"Okay, I'm here with everything you need for a fight with your boyfriend!"

I looked up from under my blanket with cats laying all over me to see Ava standing with a pizza and a huge Hershey chocolate bar.

"I see I'm too late," Ava said, setting the pizza and chocolate on the coffee table. Bobbi Jo immediately jumped up and laid her tiny little bob-tailed body on the hot pizza box for warmth.

"Huh?"

"You've got chocolate all over your chin."

I pulled the Hershey wrapper out from under the blanket, wadded it up, and threw it on the table, causing Bobbi Jo to jump from the pizza box to swat at the new toy she just found. Lenny jumped off my lap and joined her in a game of swat-the-wrapper across the floor.

"Ugh, I feel sick from eating all that chocolate."

"So, he's pretty angry about the ramp?"

"I mean, I ate the chocolate waiting for the call. But, yeah, he's definitely furious. And he was really hostile. He brought up Lydia—er, maybe I brought up Lydia. I don't know. It's a blur."

"Why on earth would you bring up Lydia and throw that in his face when he's already ticked off?"

"I thought you came over to be on my side," I said, reaching for the pizza box and grabbing a piece. Then I froze.

"You ordered pizza from M&M's?" I asked in amazement.

"Yeah, this situation demands the best pizza in town."

"But it's Mick's restaurant."

"Yeah, hence 'best pizza in town.'"

"But it's *Mick's restaurant*," I sang in disbelief. "So, his delivery guy will tell him he sent a pizza to his girlfriend's best friend, and Mick will know you came to console me after our fight, meaning he'll know I told you all about it."

"*Are you kidding me right now?* First off, that is a *stretch*. Second, he should be thankful for the business!"

I shook my head, "He's a detective, Ava, he'll know. Trust me, after the cases he's solved—this will be nothing for him to figure out. Also, I think he's good with money."

"Back to Lydia—why?"

"Yeah, I think I was the one to bring her up. He was yelling at me and making me feel dumb. I mean, yeah, I feel dumb now, but seriously, I just found everything out today. He could have told me, and he chose not to—but she knew, and it irks me SO much! And don't even—I know it's petty, you don't have to tell me. I just want to throw a pie in her face or something that can embarrass her and not hurt her or the baby."

Ave eyeballed me skeptically.

"What? I'm not a monster!"

"Okay, take a breath. He's dealing with a lot. He's angry now, but he'll get past it, and eventually, you two will do what you always do, which is fight, flirt, fight, flirt, then finally be honest with each other and make up and then you will finally stop annoying me."

I ate a second piece of pizza, contemplating everything Ava just said.

"See, you aren't refusing the pizza! It's a good thing I ordered it!"

"Speaking of pizza, I heard that Stella is working part-time for Ralph from Ralph's New York style Pizza Shop."

"How do you know that?"

"Peggy told me. I guess Peggy and Ralph have been dating the last couple of months."

"You know, it's weird you mention her. I was thinking about Bradley and how much of a tech geek he is and how much of a techy-nerd Peggy's friend Gemma is—don't you think those two would make a cute couple?"

Peggy and Gemma had a friendship similar to Ava and me, except they each owned a shop in Tri-

City. Peggy ran Peggy's Pies and Purses, and Gemma owned Gemma's Bohemian Jewelry. Their shops were next door to each other and the best friends had an adjoining door put in the back to each other's shops.

Those two ladies were a world of help last May when we had a bizarre online stalking/murder case to solve, and both Ava and I found ourselves becoming closer to both of them.

"I suppose they would be a cute couple. Don't you think we should mind our own business, though?"

"I happen to know for a fact that they will both have a booth at the festival, and Bradley is going to have a booth for the local online paper. So, I may have set it up where Gemma's jewelry booth is next to *The Village Herald*'s booth."

"Yeah, I have my own issues to work through. I think I'll stay out of this one, let you handle it while I see if I can get Mick talking to me again by the time the festival rolls around." I reached out and ripped off half the wrapper to the second family-sized Hershey bar.

I wasn't able to sleep very well after my argument with Mick, and two colossal chocolate bars washed down with most of a large pepperoni-and-extra-cheese pizza wasn't helping matters. I tossed and turned for the better part of three hours, continually looking at the clock willing it to be time to get ready for work. All four cats loved to snuggle with me in bed every night, and normally, I enjoyed their warm, furry bodies and listening to them purr as I fell asleep. Tonight, their cuddles made me feel claustrophobic, and they were less than thrilled with my tossing and turning.

By three a.m. I had had enough and got up, showered, and got ready for work. I texted Ava to let her know I was going in early to prep, knowing she was sleeping soundly and wouldn't see it until she awoke.

I walked to my car and stopped momentarily, taking in my surroundings. It was quiet, and the weather was crisp, yet I felt something sinister in the air. I shivered and felt goosebumps go up and down my body as I crossed my arms and hunched up for warmth. In the past, I wouldn't have given it a second thought, but with everything that has happened in the last two years, I've learned to trust my instincts more.

Arriving at the restaurant, I sat in the car momentarily, looking around to be sure I was safe, then I sprinted around to the back through the alley to enter, where I could turn the alarm off. Nothing happened. I'd had enough scary events take place to be cautious when I was out alone at night.

Turning the alarm off, flipping on the lights in the back, and getting into my opening routine helped to calm my nerves. I began setting up my station to make the sweet popovers for the breakfast crowd while prepping for the savory popovers for lunch. I loved my mini cast irons with the bohemian-style covers Delilah had knit herself to keep customers from burning their hands.

My mind began to wonder about Mick's condition as my body went on autopilot, preheating the oven and greasing the cast-iron muffin pans with butter, then shoving them into the oven. Preheating pans makes the perfect popover.

I'd begun coming up with a few more questions to ask Dr. Delagada the next time I saw her. I'd like to ask Meiser, but I wasn't sure he'd want to discuss this with me right now. The doctor had mentioned something about PML, and I looked it up but didn't understand it that well. There was something I wrote down about "JC positive."

I started measuring to combine the flour and salt to make fifty popovers, hoping that would be a good start for breakfast, and I could use some extras left over for lunch too. I grabbed a separate large bowl for my wet ingredients, cracking and then beating the eggs as I thought about the little I knew about PML. All I knew is that it had something to do with the new medicine he would start, and measuring levels of something, and it could cause a viral disease of the brain. I didn't know what that meant, but I'd like to know.

I realized the eggs were foamy, so I stirred in the milk, then began mixing in the wet ingredients a bit at a time to the huge bowl of dry ingredients. I grabbed the black cat oven mitts that Ava bought for us.

After getting her three kittens a few months ago, she had turned into a black cat queen, buying everything she could find. I pulled the muffin pans out and began to pour the batter into each pan, then looked at the time. We'd be opening within the hour, and Ava would be showing up soon.

I grabbed a jar of Jebidiah's Homemade Jam. He was a local business owner, a jack-of-all-trades, who was about three years older than me. His sister Jacqueline graduated with our crew, but she had gone to college to be a doctor and would be coming back to town to practice, last I heard within the year. I planned to add some strawberry, orange marmalade, and blueberry jam to some of the popovers for breakfast. I'd learned the hard way I needed to add the jams myself and offer a small sample for extras to the older residents of Leavensport—some of them were making off with whole jars of jam. I wouldn't be surprised at all if my own grandmother was one of the culprits!

I heard someone moving around up front. The lights snapped on, and Ava came through our push doors to the kitchen, wearing her curly black hair large, a short jean skirt with neon-green tights, black leather slug boots, and a bright-orange sweater with chunky beaded jewelry.

"Couldn't sleep, huh?"

"Nope, at least I'm ahead of the game this morning. The popovers will be ready as we open."

"More popovers? Didn't you just make them a few days ago? I remember that not-so-funny joke you told."

"Oh, yeah, I guess I did." I shrugged. "Oh well, I'll switch up the savory for lunch and add a different side dish," I said, feeling not much of anything. Usually, I'd be bothered by this type of mess-up, but today I just couldn't care. I popped the tray back in the oven.

"You're still off your game. Is it Meiser?"

"Yeah, also, I had one of those weird feelings coming in this morning."

Ava didn't seem surprised. "Me too. I don't like it. This woman's intuition thing."

"Me neither."

Ava headed up to unlock, and I heard our front door start to jingle, letting me know we must have had customers waiting to get in. I would guess at least five of them. We had regulars waiting to visit and have their morning coffee and Danishes every morning of the week. There were several residents of Leavensport that showed up to meet and chat at Cast Iron Creations so regularly that I could set my clock to them. I also liked that adding the little bench and library was bringing in a younger crowd from the college recently.

I had everything ready to go and decided to take some popovers up to put on display. I walked up front and used the tongs to place the rolls in our small old-fashioned pastry display case on the counter.

"Will you go around with decaf for me?" Ava called in my direction. I nodded and walked toward her to grab the pot. Just as I did, we both froze as we saw Mayor Nalini, my Aunt Fern, and Lahiri sitting at a table together. Lahiri was involved in the entire mess from last May with the murder in our online cooking class, and the whole horrific situation.

"Um, hey, anyone need decaf here?" I avoided looking at Lahiri.

"Jolie, you remember Lahiri." Aunt Fern threw it right out there to take an awkward situation and make it worse.

"Yep, sure do." I reached down and poured decaf into all three cups, whether they wanted it or not, then whirled around and headed for the kitchen.

When I walked into the kitchen, Carlos was there to greet me. "Hey, I didn't think you were due in so early?"

"Yes, I prepare for my Heavens to Murgatroyd Cast Iron Queso dip for evening time," said Carlos with a smile. "I bought fresh ingredients to drop off."

"Oh, that one is too easy for me—Snagglepuss because—"

"He's a cougar," Carlos finished for me.

"I was going to say cat, but you are right—he's a cougar."

"Miss Jolie, I meet with you and Miss Ava tomorrow. You do not forget?"

"Right, we'll meet you here. You're worrying me, making this all official, Carlos. Have we done something wrong? Are you okay?"

"No need for you to worry, Miss Jolie. I must go now. I see you soon for evening work, then tomorrow we talk."

"Was that Carlos who just left in such a hurry?" Ava asked, walking back to grab more jam for the popovers.

"Yes, he has me worried. He's adamant we both meet him privately tomorrow so he can talk to us, and he is back to calling us Miss Jolie and Miss Ava."

"That can't be good."

That night, I was resting with a glass of sweet red wine and a little dark chocolate. Only a couple of pieces tonight after my last encounter with Hershey. My cell rang, and I hoped it was Meiser. I thought about calling him all day, but I knew that Zacharia and his crew would have gone to take the ramp out. I was being stubborn and waiting for him to call me since he was the one doing so much yelling.

Unfortunately, it wasn't him; it was Lydia. Had she not been ready to squeeze that baby out the last time I saw her, I wouldn't have answered.

"Hey, Lydia. You okay?" I asked, unenthusiastically, knowing why she was calling.

Since Lydia was a nurse, she didn't want to take Lamaze classes. Mick told her she really should get the entire experience, and that *having* a baby was probably a completely different than helping *others* have babies. Lydia mentioned that she felt weird not having a partner, and Mick, being the stand-up guy he is, offered to help her out. Long story short, since Lydia and I were attempting to play nice, she called after every session—I think because it made her feel better to let me know nothing was going on with her and Mick.

"Yep, tonight was our last class. I thought I'd let you know. And I—" Lydia hesitated for what seemed like several minutes "—well, I appreciate how great you've been allowing Meiser to be my partner. That really means a lot to me."

That last bit was barely a whisper. I knew how hard it had to be for her to say that. "I didn't allow him to do anything, Lydia, he's his own man. He makes his decisions."

"Come on, we may have had our feuds, but I think we can both agree that if you didn't want that man to be my Lamaze partner he would not do it. He's over the moon for you."

"I'm not so sure about that right now."

"You didn't do anything wrong. I've been a nurse long enough to see this kind of thing happen before with couples who aren't married but are close. He should have told you everything. You are struggling with guilt because of his relapse. He's feeling sorry for himself and taking it out on you. I hate to tell you both this, but it's not a new story."

"Wow, it's like you're in my head." I bit my lower lip.

"Yeah, I told him he's acting like an idiot. You know, he can't get too mad at me with this baby about ready to pop out. I have diplomatic immunity for now."

I giggled. "Well, it makes me happy that you called him an idiot. I don't know what to say or do or how to act. I have so many questions."

"Dr. Delagada is great. Didn't she answer all your questions?"

"She answered some and explained a lot. But she mentioned something called PML because of the new medicine he'd be taking. She didn't explain, and Mick said he'd talk to me about it, but of course, he got angry before I could get any information out of him. I looked it up, but—"

"But it's confusing. Yeah, it stands for Progressive Multifocal Leukoencephalopathy. Some MS patients get it, and others don't. He tested JC negative the other day, so they'll start him on Tysabri. Next, they'll monitor to see how he does on it. They will have to check him regularly to see if he is JC positive or negative. You are rooting for negative because then he doesn't have to worry if the virus affecting his brain. MS causes lesions on the brain."

"Right, but I didn't know it was a virus?"

"Most people have the John Cunningham virus, but it's not dangerous to them. Those with MS have compromised immune systems, so if they get the virus, it can attack the brain and create more lesions. The virus would attack the cells in the brain that makes myelin. That's a protective insulating layer that forms around the nerves. If that happens, then that is when PML happens. It can cause weakness, blindness, nerve damage, and, worst-case scenario, is paralysis. I know you don't want to hear that but—"

"No, you are right. I don't *want* to hear it but I *need* to hear it. So, he is experiencing weakness now. Does that mean we should be worried about PML?"

"Not necessarily. He has MS. He will have flare-ups and relapses. It's the nature of the disease and everyone's body reacts differently."

"Yeah, the doctor was very adamant about him not using the wheelchair unless he absolutely has to. I didn't know that until I went. I thought I was helping with the ramp," Oy, I was biting my lip again—it was sure to be bleeding soon.

"Again, you didn't do anything wrong. I should probably tell you he didn't do anything wrong either. He's not used to being physically weak. This is his first major setback since he found out it was MS. He's bound to lash out while he works to adjust."

"I know. I need to call him."

"I don't think you need to worry about that."

"Why?" Just then my doorbell rang. "Oh, my—"

"Yep, my cue to take off. Hey, real quick, thanks again. You are dealing with a lot and he is too. If you want to know anything, just call. Seriously."

"Thanks, Lydia. You're not as bad as I thought."

Lydia chuckled. "Right back atcha."

I opened the door and Mick stood on my stoop with a bouquet of mixed fresh flowers. He was using his cane, which made me happy.

"Hi," I said, reaching for the brightly colored bunch of flowers.

Mick whipped his head around when hearing someone pushing through the bushes. Ava.

"Whoops, don't mind me," Ava said, putting a hand up and walking backwards, only to trip as she fell into the bushes she just came through.

"Did you enjoy our pizza last night?" Meiser called out.

"Um, yeah, I mean, Jolie ate most of it herself," she said, catching her balance.

I glared at her backside as she began moving back through the bushes, then said, "I *told* you he'd find out."

"Gotta go!" She sped through the bush and out of sight.

"So, yeah, she knows everything," I said, holding the door open for him then walking to the kitchen to grab a vase, cut the stems, and put them in lukewarm water on the island. "These are nice, thank you."

"It's the least I could do seeing that I was such an idiot." He limped, using the cane, and sat on a stool at the island. I started the cappuccino machine we bought to have here for when he stayed over, knowing he wouldn't turn it down.

"Yeah, Lydia just told me what an idiot you were." I had my head bent and looked up with a smirk.

"So, I guess I have to get used to this small-town lifestyle of whenever I get a hangnail expect the entire town to know within twenty-four hours, huh?"

"Not true at all, it only takes a good six hours for things to circulate around here."

We both stared at each other intently for a moment then laughed.

"We're getting better at this—not as much fight, flirt, fight, flirt—more quickly fight, make-up," I said, sidling up between his legs to lay my head on his chest for a hug.

"Ava said that," Mick said. He was beginning to know us way too well.

"I'm sorry about the ramp. If it makes you feel any better, I tried to get them to stop after I went to see Dr. Delagada with you and they were supposed to put a ramp in here too but I stopped that in time," I said, pulling away and batting my eyelashes, using my womanly wiles.

"I know, and they took it out today. I should have been sharing things sooner."

"Yeah, well, we both are pretty stubborn and dumb a lot too, come to think of it."

"Speak for yourself," he said with a sultry smile and taking his index finger and tapping my nose.

"Okay then, speaking for myself, you are right, you are the one who is stubborn and dumb!" I squealed a huge laugh as he lunged for me and started tickling my sides—I was a wimp when being tickled since childhood.

"No, I give, I GIVE!" I yelled, "I need to get our cappuccinos."

"Yeah, you put them in to-go cups and carry them up to the bedroom. That'll give me and my cane a head start."

I liked the way he thought.

The next morning, Ava and I went in an hour earlier than usual for the private meeting with Carlos. We drove separately because I was running late from being up late last night.

"You two are gross," Ava said when I came in with bags under my eyes.

Carlos and Ava were waiting for me, and both had coffee, but one of them had made my Chai tea and had it in a pot with cream and sugar and a cup next to it.

"Thanks," I said, sitting down to pour out the tea and add my fixins. I took a huge sip for a quick jolt of caffeine. I was afraid I might need it.

"So, what is your news?" Ava asked Carlos while looking over at me and rubbing the back of her neck. Neither of us thought this was going to be good news.

"Um, right. Miss—"

"Nope, 'Ava' and 'Jolie' is what you call us, Carlos," Ava said, leaning back in her chair and crossing her arms.

"Sorry, yes, Ava and Jolie, this is difficult for me. I can't thank you both enough for everything you have done for me. You both supported me when I needed it, and I learned so much from both of you. I have to tell you that I am buying a plot of the land for sale to start my own Mexican restaurant." Carlos gazed at his hands in his lap with a mournful expression.

Ava and I looked at each other long and hard, then both said in unison, "Carlos, that is AMAZING!"

Well, we didn't say the exact same thing, but similar accolades.

"Yes?" Carlos questioned.

"Of course, we are nothing but happy for you, and we will continue to root you on—I mean, no, we don't want to lose you, but we'd never want to hold you back either," I said as Ava enthusiastically nodded in agreement.

Carlos let out a huge sigh of relief. "That is so good for me to hear from you both. I so worried you both be upset with me and I've not wanted to tell you. I'd love to stay here and continue to work while I get the restaurant built, and I'd be willing to help find and train a replacement too. Only if you want."

"Of course, we will keep you here as long as we can, and that would be a huge help to us for you to sit in on interviews and train your replacement. I imagine Jolie and I could even pay you a bit extra for training someone." Ava looked questioningly at me, and I nodded.

"You have to be ecstatic," I said.

"Yes, I decide to call it Carlos' Hot Tamales. I had to take loan for this, but I know it is worth it."

"LOVE it," Ava barked in excitement.

"Me too, and you have the best Mexican recipes. You will do fabulous."

"Thank you. You two will be guest of honor and be with me during ribbon-cutting ceremony," Carlos said.

"Oh-la-la, ribbon cutting?" Ava eyed me with her huge brown eyes.

"Yes, I will be first in family to own a business. I plan to do a big grand opening. You and Jolie will be guests of honor."

"Well, the pleasure is ours, Carlos. Now, do you have a time estimated for starting the business?" I asked.

"That was one reason why I waited to tell. I had trouble at first with financing but found a good partner to help with the loan. He says business can open by spring, which is good time to start business."

I didn't like the sound of that. I wanted to ask him who his partner was. I hoped no one was taking advantage of him. I know Carlos had complained about finances a lot to Ava and me, and it helped him a lot when we were able to afford to make him an assistant manager. Still, it wasn't my business, so I bit my tongue.

"Okay, well, I come back later for my shift. I let you two get set up." Carlos stood, and we stood to hug him with one more congratulations.

After he left, Ava looked at me, "So, I saw that look. You're concerned too?"

"Yep, but we should mind our business with this, otherwise we risk looking like we aren't being supportive."

Later that week, I was having dinner with Mick at his restaurant out on the patio. It was a cool fall evening and the sun was setting. Mick had added a fire pit further beyond the patio late this summer, and since this was the first he was using ithe wanted to be present to make sure all went well. It was a picturesque view overlooking the fields and the woods behind them with all the leaves changing colors.

"This is so nice." I sipped my tea and savored my Tiramisu.

"Yep, I think these will work out. I like that Zacharia added the iron grates over them and took several safety precautions. It's a risk trying this because I had to pay more for insurance. We'll see how it works out."

"So, you did this expecting to be spending more time working at the restaurant. Is that still your plan? Have you talked to Teddy about all of this?" I asked.

"I talked to him yesterday for quite some time about my relapse, and I let him know that things could be hit or miss at times. He told me he's willing to work with me. He has to look into some insurance and legal issues to protect himself. I get that. In the meantime, while he's figuring all that out, yes, I'll spend more time working here for now. Also, you'll be happy to know I filled that prescription for Lexipro and started on it, and I talked to Tabitha about making an appointment."

"So, that's not a conflict of interest?"

"Well, not right now. I made an appointment to help me sort out a few things. We both agreed that I might need to have her recommend someone else at some point, and we'll deal with it when we get there."

"Well, good. That's progress I—" I looked up, interrupted by hearing people shouting from across the lane by the B&B. "Who is that?"

"Hold on," Mick said, getting up and going inside then coming back out with his binoculars he kept to look at the birds in the park nearby.

"Whoever it is, bushes are blocking my view. I can't tell right now. They don't sound happy, though."

"Wait, that sounds like one of the Zimmerman brothers," I said.

"Yep, I can see him now. He's talking to that tall guy you were talking to at the farmers market. He's from the city—what's his name?"

"Ralph, the pizza guy?" I asked.

"Yeah, there's some pushing going on now. Maybe I should drive over," he said, looking down at his cane, knowing driving would be faster. I pushed my seat out to go with him, and we moved toward his truck. Then the scuffle ended as Ralph jumped in a little red car and sped off as Zed stomped toward his pickup truck.

"Guess they didn't need us to intervene," I said, going around to his other side to hold his hand as we moved back to our table.

"Well, you weren't done with your dessert anyway," he grinned.

"Has Lydia said anything to you about who the father of the baby is yet?" I took a large bite of my Tiramisu, leaning toward him.

Mick's eyes widened, and he looked around quickly. "Oh—hey, Bradley!" he yelled out. Bradley was toward the middle of the parking lot quite far from us for Mick to say hello.

Wait, was that? Yes, Lahiri was walking next to him!

"Oh, hi," Bradley said, picking up his pace to get closer to us as Lahiri tried to keep up.

"Hi," Lahiri said, looking at the ground.

"You two having dinner together?" Mick asked, which seemed unusual to me. Usually, I'm the nosey one, and he doesn't care at all who is dating who.

"Um, yeah, Lahiri wrote an article for *The Village Herald*, and I asked if she wanted to grab a bite with me." It was Bradley's turn to look down awkwardly, avoiding eye contact with me.

"Are you both ready for the festival to start?" Bradley was grasping at topics of conversation.

"Sure thing," I said in a clipped voice, taking a sip of tea.

"Mkay, well, we have a reservation, so," Bradley said.

"Enjoy," Mick said, waving.

"I didn't know those two were an item," I said.

"I don't think they are together. Sounds like she did some work for him and they're just grabbing dinner."

"A reservation?"

"Good point. Speaking of the festival and full disclosure—"

Uh-oh, this didn't sound promising.

"My parents and Miles and my sister are coming to the festival."

I almost choked on my tea. "Why?" I managed to spit out. Mick had called off our relationship last Thanksgiving because he was concerned about me being in danger. His family was involved with the Sicilian mafia, and he had changed his name to get into law enforcement and break ties with them. To hear they were visiting was a total shock.

"Well, you know that my sister, Maria, and I have been mailing letters back and forth for years. After everything went down with Marty last year, Miles reached out to me again."

"Okay, I know he was mayor of Tri-City for a while, and I thought you two had an okay relationship. But you seemed bent on wanting nothing to do with Marty or your parents," I said, still trying to suppress my astonishment.

"Oh, Marty and I will not be making up in this lifetime. Believe me! Maria, Miles, and I have talked more. Especially right after everything went down with Marty, which was right when you and I weren't together, and you were in the Dominican Republic with Ava, I went undercover and went through a trial treatment for MS. A lot happened during that time, I've gotten closer to those two."

"Well, I think that sounds like a good thing," I said, truly happy for him.

"I guess. I'm still leery. Anyway, Maria and Miles have never separated themselves from my parents. So, in spending more time with my brother and sister, that meant that I started to interact more with my parents. It has been awkward, but I'm trying to make it work."

"I'm sorry," I said.

"I am too. We avoid talking about my job and their lifestyle."

"Seems appropriate."

"I'm still not sure I'm ready to act as if nothing happened," Mick said skeptically.

"I can completely understand that."

"Anyway, Maria has a big mouth. I talk about you. She told them. They want to meet you."

Oy.

Chapter Four

By six a.m. Friday morning, the little village of Leavensport was hopping. Vendors from our town, as well as Tri-City business owners, were all doing last-minute decorations and preparations for their booth. As always, a few of the older residents of the town were out bright and early, walking around before the waves of people showed up.

I had large warmer bags full of yummy breakfast and brunch foods that I put on a rolling cart to push to our booth. Ava was already there, counting our till before we opened for business. We had a few last-minute fall decorations of rust and green hanging lights we planned to hang around the booth.

Pushing the cart down the sidewalk, I saw two people standing some distance away in the middle of the sidewalk, arguing with each other. One looked to be a younger man in his twenties wearing a light beige straw fedora with a black rim. He had a long, narrow face with a scruffy, unkempt long reddish-brown beard and a mustache I found to be comical as it reminded me of an old-fashioned cartoon villain with a handlebar mustache. The other was a lady who looked to be middle-aged with cool-looking long, straight lavender hair done in pixie braids with heavy blue eye shadow, bright red lipstick, and lengthy beautifully decorated turquoise-and-brown-patterned nails. This beauty was wielding those nails as a weapon in Mr. Fedora's face.

"I don't care how much younger than me you are, son. This is my section of the festival to work. I need a lot of space to move around as I sing. Also, I don't need your sax playing overpowering my songs."

"I don't only play the saxophone." Mr. Fedora said, taking his hat off and bowing in Lavender pixie's presence. "I'm a candle maker, play sax, and I recite lyrical poetry as my Medieval ancestors did, my dear."

"Well, I'm thrilled for you. I hate to play this game, but I did get here before you, meaning I am claiming this area." Lavender Hair gestured around them with those long fingers, made lengthier by those beautiful nails.

I have to admit I was torn. Our booth was in this area, and they both looked like interesting people to watch. I'd have to find out where the other landed and go sit in on their performance later.

"Ma'am, I do understand the conundrum. It's only that my candle making booth with the candles I sell is right here, and I'm not able to move the booth on short notice," Mr. Fedora, handlebar mustache man said, nodding to his candle booth three booths down from us.

I'd have to check that out. I *adored* burning scented candles when I was home.

During this entire scene, I was standing, observing the argument because they were blocking me from moving past them on the sidewalk. I didn't want to go into the grass with the cart any longer than I had to.

"Oh my, are we in your way, darling?" Lavender Hair asked, batting lengthy, thick eyelashes at me.

"I'm sorry. I didn't mean to interrupt this—" I stood with hands up at a loss for what exactly this was.

"No, no, allow me to introduce myself. I am Bagwell Theodore the Third, troubadour extraordinaire and this is my acquaintance—"

I thought he must know Lavender Hair's name and was getting ready to introduce me, but he looked around, then put his index and pinky fingers in his mouth and gave a shrill whistle. Out bounced a white cocker spaniel with blondish spots. It looked to be a young pup but seemed very smart at such a young age.

"Where have you been, Boo?" Bagwell asked, reaching down to rub Boo's belly as he or she rolled over. Boo then jumped up and began running circles around Lavender Hair.

"Oh my, get that little fleabag away from me!" she screamed.

"He won't hurt you, Myrtle," Bagwell said.

"So, Bagwell, you have a booth near me, it sounds like," I said, trying to break some of the tension.

"Oh, please call me Baggy—I insist."

"I didn't know you had this mutt here. I think I will move closer to the mall area where there are more clothes, and a spa booth with a nail salon. I may look into having my nails done differently each day of the festival." With that, Myrtle quickly grabbed my hand and shook it, looked at the little dog with disgust, glowered at Baggy, and sashayed off in a new direction.

"I don't think she liked me very well," Baggy said, reaching down to pick Boo up.

"Well, I need to head to my booth to get everything set up," I said, moving past him and Boo.

"What was that all about?" Ava asked, coming to meet me at the sidewalk to help move the cart across the lawn to our booth.

"Seems this year there is a performing artist named Myrtle and a troubadour named Baggy with his sidekick, Boo, the cocker-spaniel."

"Interesting," Ava said as we got to our booth.

"This looks great!" I said, taking a few steps out and pulling my phone out to get a picture as Ava posed with one hand behind her head, chin held up—a pose that helped to lengthen the neck for the best picture, she said. The booth had a custom-made banner shaped like a large apron, with our cast-iron skillet logo and what else but three black kittens down the side. Fabric patches with some of my signature family recipes written out on them dotted the apron-shaped banner here and there, making it a textile piece of art. Of course, Ava's girlfriend, Delilah, hand-crafted it.

We had what I believed was one of the prime spots in town for the festival. We were near our restaurant that was right in the art district. Most everyone who came to the festival made a point to visit this area to see what all of the kids had for sale from their art and crafts work. Delilah had the kids research different charities and then pick out three to donate the profits to. All the parents were pleased with her work, their kids' efforts, and the charitable contributions that also helped the kiddos build their social, emotional skills.

We finished hanging our fall lights around our booth and opened for business early for some of the long-time residents who wanted coffee, hot tea, and cocoa with our Danishes and fried donuts. Over a few hours, it continued to get busier, then we hit a lag as Magda and Carlos came to give us a break.

"Want to walk around a bit?" I asked Ava.

"Actually, I told Delilah I'd stop by with some food for her. She won't get much of a break. Want to come with me?"

"Nah, go ahead. I'm going to walk around a bit."

I headed east toward the Leavensport Circle to look at everything. Dr. Libby had her annual booth set up with cute cartooned pets all over her booth and stuffed animals and some of her friendly dogs and cats hanging around. She provided information on the importance of spaying and neutering pets, as well as the best ways to keep happy, healthy fur friends.

The Leavensport pool was closed but hadn't been drained for the season yet, so Tri-City's Barker Bay Boating company always had remote-controlled miniature versions of the boats they sold floating around in it, and nearby, a table of pamphlets with information on the various models for sale. The mall area was hopping, and Jeni's Diner's booth had a long line for her special double-decker triple cheeseburger and fair fries. I'd have to see if the line died down and get one of each before heading back to our booth.

"Hey, don't you run a restaurant booth? What are you doing drooling over here?"

I turned to see Mick standing in worn, light-blue jeans and a maroon cable-knit sweater. He had his cane with him but didn't seem to be using it. He appeared in good spirits, not to mention he looked super hot.

"Jeni is just like me. She gets tired of her own food and comes to our place all the time. And look who is talking. You have a restaurant and eat my cooking all the time," I said, leaning into him for a kiss and smelling his familiar spicy smell that sent shivers down my spine.

"PDA alert! Public! Display! Of! Affection! Get a room!"

Mick and I turned as I saw Gemma and Peggy walking toward us.

"I hear you have a new beau yourself, so ..." I teased Peggy, who had been heckling us.

"He and I have been together for months now. It's been too long since you and I have talked. We need to catch up," Peggy said, reaching out to hug me. As her ponytail flipped around, I could smell the strawberry-scented hair product in her strawberry-blonde hair.

Gemma looked gorgeous as always in bold-patterned yellow, green, and black skirt with a black turtleneck. Her hair was piled high up in a bun, and she sported several chunky, colorful beaded necklaces, bracelets, gemmed earrings and a sapphire nose ring.

"Ma'am, is this guy bothering you?" Gemma asked, grinning up at Meiser.

"Right, I'm so sorry, you all haven't met yet. Mick, this is Peggy of Peggy's Pies and Purses in

Tri-City, and this is Gemma of Gemma's Bohemian Jewelry store. Ladies, this is Meiser—er—Mick," I said, shaking my head.

"No worries, Jolie." Gemma looked at Mick, "she's told us so much about you that I'm sure that's why she thinks we already know you."

"Hopefully, she talked to you both when we were getting along. I've heard nothing but good things about both of you." Meiser shook hands with them.

"Oh, we were able to tell how she felt about you quite easily. Her face tells all," Peggy said, side-eying me as my face turned three shades of crimson.

Mick smiled down at me while putting an arm around me, pulling me to him and reaching down to kiss my curls.

"Well, our break is over. We'll let you two back to your PDA," Gemma said, doing a little "toodle-loo" with her finger wave.

"I like them," Mick said.

"So, where are the parents?"

"They'll be here tomorrow. I talked Carlos, Magda, and Ava into letting me spend the afternoon with you today. That way, I get you all to myself, and it gives you an out tomorrow so you don't have to spend as much time with my parents and me," he grinned.

"Win-win," I said.

Yesterday had been a fantastic start to the festival, and we had three more days ahead of us. After spending the afternoon with Mick, we had gone to my house, where he helped me prep and cook what

I could for the next day. Carlos used the kitchen at the restaurant to prep for his shifts at the festival.

This morning I was able to get to the booth more easily as Baggy had claimed his area. I had forgotten to check out Myrtle's act yesterday, so I made a mental note to do so today.

We got the hot beverages ready to go and began selling with the first customer who was a younger woman who must have been an out-of-towner. She had long, thick, wavy black hair, a distinguished mole over her thick mauve lips, fawny, smooth skin, and dark eyes.

"Cocoa, please, and I'd love extra whipped cream and some marshmallows in it too if you have them," the beauty said, smiling broadly at me.

"You sound like my kind of woman," I said, using a large spoon full of marshmallows and adding extra whipped cream.

"Seems like that his a good thing seeing that you are dating my brother." She took a sip of cocoa.

"Oh, wow, you are Meiser's sister!" Ava pushed me aside, reaching out to shake her hand.

"Who?" she asked.

Oh man, leave it to Ava. "She means Mick, sorry," I reached out to shake her hand as well.

"Hey, Maria," Mick said, walking up with two older versions of himself. They had to be his parents. He had his mother's eyes, but the lines of his face and his cheekbones came from his father.

"Hi, Meiser," his sister drew out the name in a playful tone with an ornery expression on her face.

Mick squished his lips, contorting his face as a brother would at a sister who was making his life difficult.

"Ah yes, I take it the blonde is the one who created this ridiculous Meiser name for you," the dark-haired woman eyed me indignantly.

"Mother, be nice," Mick grunted, then turned and got close to his sister's face. "See what you caused?" he murmured.

"Mamma, be good," Maria purred.

"Jolie, this is my mother, Maya, and my father, Maddox. Mamma, Papa, this is my *girlfriend*, Jolie."

"It's very nice to meet you both," I said, reaching out a hand as Maria handed money over for the cocoa. "Oh no, please, all of you are welcome to anything we offer at no cost."

"Huh?" Ava elbowed me.

I mumbled something noncoherent in her direction that sounded something like, "Shut up and do not embarrass me." I hoped she got the point.

Maria smiled sweetly at Ava, handing the money to her. "I insist. Your help is beautiful, and if nothing else, you should take this as a tip."

"Help? I'm not the help. I'm a co-owner of this restaurant," Ava said, reaching for Maria's money.

I noticed Maria's eyes lit up with an energetic fire. She seemed to enjoy Ava's spark a little too much.

"What is your name, darling?" Maria purred.

"Ava," she said, opening the till.

I reached for the money and pulled it out of her hand and returned the elbow to the side. "Seriously, thank you, but we will not accept your money this weekend."

"Well, then, if you won't accept my money, maybe you will take me on a tour of your town?" Maria pointedly asked Ava.

Ava seemed oblivious to Maria's advances, "I'm working," she scoffed like that was the dumbest thing she'd ever heard.

"We'll see," Maria said.

"Ava is in a relationship with the local artist, Delilah," Mick grunted. The way he and Maria communicated reminded me of how Ava and I argued.

"Like I said, 'we'll see,'" Maria said.

Maddox and Maya stood still in silence during this entire exchange. They had said nothing to me other than Maya's rude comment.

"Can I get either of you anything?" I offered.

"We are rather picky about the food we eat. We tend to create our pastas and sauces from scratch and only use the best oils," Maya stated, turning up her nose. "Micky, I'd love to try something from your restaurant."

"Well, Mother, Jolie is one of the best chefs in the village. I'd say in the country, but I may be biased." Mick's mother had her arm through her son's, allowing him to lead her around and looking to claim him. Mick moved around the booth toward me and put an arm around me and leaned down to kiss my curls as he usually did.

Maya's face twisted into infuriated scowls watching her son with me.

"Well, well, who is this?" my Grandma Opal cooed, hurrying toward us. She had the entire family following her, including my mom, Aunt Fern, Uncle Wylie, Tom Costello, Uncle Eddie, and his entire family—wife Shelly, three daughters—Karly, Sadie, and Serenity, with his other son, Kevin, in tow.

Suddenly I felt queasy. It was apparent Mick's parents were not thrilled with me—and here comes my clan, which would not earn me any points with them.

"This is my family." I gestured to them, hoping for the best. Mick's dad wore crisply ironed beige slacks with what looked to be designer Italian loafers, a belt, a button-up shirt, and a tie. His mother was sporting an expensive linen outfit that was off-white with gold dripping off every finger, earlobe, and around her neck.

Then there was my family with Grandma Opal in elastic-waist jeans, jelly shoes with white socks, and a sweatshirt that had a kitten on it that said, "My grandkids love me. Why? Because I told them they'd better!" The rest of my family was dressed similarly, with the men sporting flannel shirts and work boots. Maya and Maddox were smirking at my family, which bothered me a lot.

Mick made all the introductions, hugging the women in the family and shaking hands with each of the men. They all loved him, and surprisingly, he found them endearing. He loved to joke around with them. Mick knew me too well, so now, as he felt my entire body tighten when my family made their way over, I'm sure he understood that I sensed how much his parents didn't like me, so he rubbed my back and whispered in my ear, "Everything is fine. Let them all just be who they are. Everything will work out on its own. We've got each other, and they can like it or not—I mean my parents." He stated the obvious as he kissed my temple.

I looked up appreciatively at him. He really was the yin to my yang. I hoped I did the same for him.

"We are thrilled to have this young man be a part of our family," my mom, Patty, said.

"You should be. You have a Milano with you. We'd love for him to move where we are," Maya said.

"Oh, and where is it you live?" Grandma Opal asked in a not-so-pleasant tone.

"Well, it's great you asked. Currently, we are in the Ritz hotel in Tri-City, but we are looking for a home to purchase there—in the best neighborhood, of course."

I felt Mick's body tighten. I read that stress was not good for those with MS, and I wanted to discuss this with him about detective work—would he be more stressed by working or staying home? Looks like I'd have to add family to that list to discuss.

"You never told me this!" Mick said.

"Well, you didn't ask," Maddox said. "Maria will be moving, and Miles is already there, so—"

"And, Marty is close by," Mick said with a grin, knowing that would irritate his parents.

"We are not discussing him," Maddox said. "That is a private family situation."

"The Tuckers are my family. They know Marty very well—he put me in danger and Jolie saved me—he also attacked her. So I think it's fine to mention him here." Mick stared hard at his parents, daring them to say anything.

I saw many in my family look from awkward to proud to have Mick consider them family. It was my turn to rub his back.

"Well, we'll be leaving you be so you can help Ava run the booth. Looks like you're getting a bit of a line," Aunt Fern said, turning Grandma around by the elbow to get her and the rest of the family moving.

Maya took that as her cue for her and Maddox to head out.

"Well, it seems we will meet again, young lady. We will have to take the two of you out to a proper restaurant for dinner where we can all put on something a little less ... rustic," Maya said.

"Mother, I—" Mick started.

"I would love that. It's been a long time since I've had an opportunity to dress up for a lovely dinner, ma'am," I said sweetly.

"You don't have to—" Mick started.

"Well, lovely manners," Maddox said, more pleased with me as they headed off.

"I'm so sorry about that. Trust me, they are NOT moving here. I will make sure of that," Mick said, running his fingers through his thick brown locks that were starting to show signs of gray, giving him a sexy, mature look.

"Whatever happens, we'll deal with it. You've witnessed my family."

"Yeah, and unfortunately, you've witnessed mine."

Mick had stayed over last night after the family reunion. I was up bright and early, and he seemed to be hurting and weaker because of walking so much the last couple of days. He said he planned to take the wheelchair with him today but start with the cane, then move to the walker and only use the wheelchair if he had to. He was going to head to the festival later in the day, but I had to get going, so Mick said he'd take care of all the cat stuff. He had Stewart and Lucky with him, so we had the six of them there. Luckily, because all six of them were so spoiled rotten, they all got along—well, some hissing here and there, but other than that, they were fine.

I had the opportunity to walk around the festival in the morning today and got to see Myrtle's performance. I had heard Baggy play his sax. He was a beautiful jazz musician—the lyrical poetry was a tad on the cheesy side for my taste but to each their own. Myrtle had a lovely smokey alto. I kind of wished she and Baggy got along better. She was all jazz, and I thought they would make an incredible duo. I left a tip for her as I had done for Baggy, and she nodded a smile in my direction.

Heading back to our booth, I saw Mayor John Cardinal in his pristine, wrinkle-free suit and wing-tips with his Opie freckles and extra-white smile talking with his wiry, curly-haired, chain-smoking assistant, Tonya Morrison, who had seemed way too chummy with him the last time I visited their office. There was another young man with the two of them that I didn't recognize, but Betsy was chatting with him then moved away back to her booth.

I went to our booth and put my apron on, noticing that the Zed and Zander Zimmerman, local brothers that were farmers who always sported bib overalls with work boots and old T-shirts, were at Ralph's Pizza booth. The conversation seemed tense, but not hostile like the other day. I saw Betsy carrying a tray to the booth with three samples of her yummy s'more desserts. If anything could lighten the mood, it was some chocolate. At least that always worked for me!

I saw Peggy was with Gemma, and I'd heard that Stella had been working with Peggy part-time at her shop, helping her out. Peggy and Stella seemed to be watching Ralph closely as if they knew something was up, but then I got busy with orders.

I was in the middle of an order when I heard screaming coming from right outside the Community Center. I dropped my ladle as others turned to see what was happening and ran toward the yelling. Lydia was lying on the grass with her knees bent and one hand on her rounded stomach. She was quiet for a moment, then she closed her eyes and her face twisted as she screamed again . . . Mick must have gotten there at some point. He had rolled close to her in his wheelchair and was leaning out of it, holding her hand. I heard a siren moving down the sidewalk—the hospital was very close, and it looked like one of Lydia's co-workers had put a siren on a golf cart to get through the crowd faster.

I began looking around in a bit of a panic, not knowing whether I should go to them since Meiser was there or stay put. I saw Ralph grab his neck as if he was choking. I was the only one that saw him because everyone's attention was on Lydia. I started toward him. As I got closer, all of the color drained from his face. Suddenly, he collapsed behind his booth. I gasped, then sprinted the rest of the way. I ran around the side of the booth and knelt by his side. "HELP!" I screamed as I leaned over him, holding his face in my hands.

Ralph's eyes flew open, and he grabbed my sweater. "More---S—MORES in the sun," he gurgled. Then he was gone.

Chapter Five

"The festival is ruined! How dare she go into labor and that horrific man die during our annual festival!" Mrs. Dalton spewed.

The Daltons were a thirty-ish couple in the village that loved to remind all of us that they were superior to anyone in a small village.

"I know, they truly ruined everything for everyone, D-A-R-L-I-N-G!" Ava exaggerated, holding a hand over her forehead as if she would faint any moment, then glared at Mrs. Dalton. "You are one of the craziest people I've ever met. You walk around this town like you somehow own it and all of us in it. We don't work for you. Lydia is in labor as we speak. A man died. So sorry if that is an inconvenience to your life!"

"Whoa, relax there, slugger," I said, holding Ava back.

Mrs. Dalton jerked her neck back with a look that screamed, "WELL-I-NEVER!" And then spun around on her stiletto heels and grabbed her city-lawyer-husband's arm, strutting off in a huff.

Chief Teddy Tobias had cordoned off the area where I had stood over Ralph.

"Aren't you going to help Teddy?" I asked Mick. It had been a few hours since the chaos. Mick had gone to the hospital with Lydia and had just returned. Teddy said the entire festival area was closed at least for the rest of today and maybe longer, depending on what he found while processing the scene.

"We are still in a gray area about if I'm working there or not. Are you ready to go home?" He seemed to be reverting into his depression. Things had been looking up there for a few days.

"Teddy told me to stick around until he's done doing all of his police thingys. I assume because I was there when it happened. You know, Ralph did say something to me before he passed away." I knew this would be bait that the detective in Mick couldn't resist.

"Okay, do you mind if I head home? I'm beat. I see Ava is still here so she can take you home after you talk to Teddy." He used his arms to turn his wheelchair around.

I willed my jaw not to fall open. "Hey—"

Mick turned back to me.

"I heard Lydia had the baby at the hospital. Do you know what she named him?" I wanted to ask what was going on, but I chickened out last minute.

"Monty. It's the name of Mick's great grandfather. Lydia seems to have excellent taste in names like she does men." Maya Milano came sauntering out of nowhere and put her hands on the handles of the wheelchair of her son. "I can drive you home, son. We'll come back for your truck later."

Mick saw my shocked look and I saw the sting of pain cross his face as she pushed him away. My mind began racing, and that old feeling of a pounding heart and a murky mind came spinning back. I took in a couple of gulps for breaths. Watching Ralph die before my eyes while seeing Mick with Lydia and hearing she named the baby after his great grandfather had me seeing double. I stumbled and almost fell over except someone caught me.

"Whoa, are you okay?" Keith asked.

"No," I sucked in a breath, trying not to cry.

"Teddy wants to talk to you. Let me see if I can have him hold off a minute. Here, come sit on the bench." Keith led me to the nearby bench then grabbed a bottled water from a nearby vendor who was packing up. "Drink this and take deep breaths. I'll be right back."

Keith had been my high school boyfriend. He wasn't thrilled when Mick and I began our on-and-off relationship. Still, I didn't know where Ava was, and I was happy someone was there for me now.

"Okay, Teddy said I could bring you over in a few minutes. Do you want to talk about it, or do you want me to go find you some chocolate or both?" He grinned.

That made me smile. I took a few gulps of the water then said, "I'd love to talk about it, but I don't think that would be fair to you."

"I'm assuming it's a Mick thing then." He looked down at his hands as he spread his fingers and cracked his knuckles—something he always did when he was uncomfortable.

"It's everything. Every time I think I'm making a few big strides forward, something or multiple things happen that make me feel that I'm retreating further back."

"*C'est la vie*," he said, reciting something Madame Glander, our high school French teacher, would say all the time.

"Ah, *oui*," I replied and laughed.

"Okay, thanks. Believe it or not, you helped just by being here in the moment. Let's go talk to Teddy."

"Hi, Jolie, as always, you seem to be around when these things happen," Teddy said with his muscular arms crossed around his chest. Teddy was short and stocky but hit the gym regularly. He was the youngest man ever to make chief in Leavensport, but his dad and his grandpa were both chief, and his dad died young of cancer like my step-dad did.

"It's not like I planned it," I said palms facing the sky. "How's Shirley doing?"

"Aw, she's doing great. Poor thing, I had her outside playing fetch with her and she got a burr stuck in her paw. You know, that German Shepard whined like a baby. I thought it had to be something worse, but Dr. Libby said she just had it really jammed in there, so we got that taken care of and she's good as new."

"Probably won't want to play catch for a while, though."

"Are you kidding? I brought her home and the first thing she did was grab the tennis ball and bring it to me!" He exclaimed, laughing heartily.

"That sounds about right," Keith said.

"Okay, so, how is it you were by Ralph?"

"I was caught up with all the Lydia having a baby drama. I looked around frantically and noticed he was pale and he was clutching his throat."

"Was anyone else there with him?"

"No."

"Had you seen anyone with him right before everything happened? Your booth was across from his."

Oy, I had seen the Zimmerman brothers and Betsy. All of them were my friends, and I sure as heck didn't want to make them into suspects.

"Who did you see?" Keith asked. Unfortunately, just like he could help me in a time of need, he also knew what my facial expressions meant.

I sighed, "I mean, I saw Zed and Zander Zimmerman talking to him, and then Betsy brought the three of them some sample desserts. But he had people there off and on all day."

"Were they all the last ones you remember seeing with him?" Teddy asked as Keith wrote it all down.

"Yeah, but I got busy, so, anyone else could have shown up."

"Why isn't Detective Meiser here?" Keith asked, looking around.

"He quit," Teddy said.

Now my jaw did drop.

"What did you just say?"

Teddy's neck began to blotch, and his freckles all looked like they were connecting the dots. "You didn't know?"

"He told me you two were making some decisions about this," I said, hands on hips.

Keith looked nervous.

"I don't think I should say any more," Teddy said, taking his boot and moving the toe around the grass.

"Is there anything else you think we need to know?" Keith asked, changing the subject.

"Um, well, last week, Mick and I saw the Zimmerman brothers in a heated argument with Ralph, but we don't know what it was about. They looked more civil today, though. Other than that, I know he was dating Peggy."

"She has the pie shop, right?"

"Yes."

"Do you know if he had pie today?" Keith asked.

"How would I know that? I saw him eating Betsy's dessert."

"So, you did see him eat that then?" Teddy looked hard at Keith.

"Yeah, why? He seemed very young to have a heart attack or something like that. Do you know what happened to him yet?"

"No, we have to wait on the autopsy. If you think of anything else—"

"Oh my gosh. This may be nothing, but you should know. I can't believe this slipped my mind!"

"What's that?"

"He grabbed my sweater and whispered something to me—but I couldn't make it all out."

I told Teddy and Keith what I thought he said, and Keith wrote it down, and then I headed home.

When I pulled in the drive, I was exhausted from all the events of the entire weekend, particularly today. Ava came out of her door, waving frantically at me.

"I have to go in and take a long hot bath and get some chocolate and a glass of red wine," I said, dragging myself toward my door.

"Oh no, you don't. Peggy is here and she needs us!"

Crap! Double crap! I'm a horrible friend. I even told Teddy that she was dating Ralph, but I didn't think to look for her to comfort her. I was too caught up in my messed up life. I made a beeline for Ava.

"I have wine and chocolate here," she whispered as I passed her.

I walked into Ava's brick-red living room with zebra-printed furniture and white bookshelves with black cat statues all over them. Peggy and Gemma were both holding the three kittens. Kitten love is the perfect thing when you are grieving.

"Hey, I'm so sorry it took me this long to find you," I said, collapsing on the couch next to her and grabbing her for a hug.

Peggy squeezed me tightly, and I felt her body shake as she cried. I felt tears stinging my eyes and looked at Gemma, who had tears streaming down her face. I knew she ached seeing her best friend in so much pain.

"Meeeewwww," cried one of the babies.

"Whoops, sorry, sweetie," Peggy released me and picked up Lily to kiss her head, then Ava came over and scooped her up and sat in her rounded, neon-green-cushioned wicker chair.

"Where were you?" Peggy asked.

"Talking to the chief," I said, then I filled them in on everything I knew so far.

"Yeah, I have to go in to speak to him tomorrow. Ralph has been acting off the last month or so, but I don't know why. You know Stella has been working for him part-time, and she helps me out from time to time too. I talked him into hiring her, and at first, the two of them didn't get along so well, but I think they were warming up to each other lately," Peggy reached for another tissue and blew her nose.

"I hate that you have to go through this," Gemma said, laying a hand on her knee.

"Well, I don't have to go through it alone. I'm officially hiring the two of you to investigate his death." Peggy looked from Ava to me.

"Whoa, I'm not licensed like Ava," I said, sitting back.

"Yeah, but you are listed on the website, and I trust you," Peggy said.

"She's listed because somehow she always knows what to do. Let's call her my assistant to make it all legal," Ava waggled her eyebrows at me.

I looked at Peggy's large sad eyes and couldn't say no.

The next morning I went to Mick's house to talk to him about everything. I knocked and got no answer, so I called his cell.

"Hey," he picked up.

"Where are you?" I asked.

"At the hospital with Lydia and Monty."

I didn't like how unhappy that made me.

"Aw, okay, I'll let you go then," I said.

"Why, where are you?"

"At your place. I wanted to talk about something I heard."

"What did you hear?"

"Probably not best to discuss on the phone. Plus, you're in the middle of a visit." I couldn't hide the edge in my voice.

"So, now you're mad that I'm visiting Lydia and the baby?"

"What do you mean *now*?"

"You seem to be mad a lot lately."

"Well, I don't appreciate someone who knows I have trust issues and then flat-out lies to my face after telling me that we are all in this thing together," I spat out.

"So you know I quit."

"I know you quit."

Long silence.

"Jolie, are you still there?"

"Yes, I said the last thing—waiting for you to explain now."

I heard a long, annoyed sigh. "A lot is happening right now. You had a time when you needed space to figure things out. Now, I need time to figure things out."

"What does that mean?" I asked, watching Stewart and Lucky looking at me from the window as Stewart put a paw on the window.

"It means I think we should take a little space while I work through some things."

I felt like eight archers stood right in front of me, aiming at my heart as I heard eight SWISH sounds, each dart hit me directly in the heart.

Chapter Six

"Come on, let's set up our I Spy Slides to take your mind off Meiser. He'll regret what he said in a day or two if he hasn't already," Ava said, handing over a cup of coconut chai hot tea with sweetener and milk to help soothe my soul.

"I don't know. He's been all over the place the last month. He's not himself, and now his family is moving here. That's why he wanted a break last Thanksgiving—so that is not going to help me at all. I'm not sure what I can do at this point." My sip of tea wasn't soothing me fast enough, so I gulped and felt the burn going down my throat.

"Okay, time to focus on what we are being paid for," Ava said.

"So, you are paying me too, then, right?"

"Not as much as the fee I charge, but yes, you will receive a little something. I mean, you are not a professional PI yet."

"Ava, how are you a professional PI? I looked up what has to be done. When did you spend time on a police force?"

"Um, when we were in high school, and we worked as security guards at the mall. That counts. And since you worked there too, that means you just need to take some courses, fill out the forms, take the test, and pay the fee—then *voila*—we co-own a second business, and you get paid more. I guess you didn't read all the fine print! Not to mention, I got Tabitha to write a letter vouching for me. We'll get her to do one for you too. I think that is what cinched it."

I laughed under my breath at that last bit of information about Tabitha. I knew it was something like that. "Okay, whatever. Pay me what you think is fair. I'm interested in helping Peggy figure this out, and I need to have something to take my mind off Mick while he figures all this out."

"So, let's start with a list of suspects first. It's a good thing you were there when it happened. We want to note who we saw around him."

"We don't know that he was murdered yet, Ava. It could have been a heart attack. I think our first task is to see if we can find out what the coroner report says."

"I already know. He was poisoned. Teddy asked Betsy come in to talk to him tomorrow because her s'more dessert was the last thing he ate."

"How do you know that?"

"Because I'm a licensed PI. I keep telling you to get your license!"

"It doesn't matter that you are a licensed PI, Ava. Teddy is not just going to hand over that information to you," I said, exhausted with her.

"No, but he did call Peggy in to let her know, who then contacted the PI she hired," Ava grinned.

"Oh, wow, so it's official then. Okay, well, I didn't see any blood or anything, so I thought it could be a heart attack, or he choked on something or had a brain thingy," I said.

"An aneurism?" Ava rolled her eyes at me.

"Um, yes—sorry, I couldn't think of the word!"

"Poisoned. They think Betsy did it? How could Teddy think that? We all grew up together, plus those two have some sort of secret crush on each other!" Ava looked mortified at the thought.

"It's his job to look into everyone, as it's our job now, Ava." I paced back and forth, thinking about what to have her type. "Right, okay, write down what it sounded like he said to me. It sounded like 's'mores in the sun,' which was what I saw Betsy bring him right before he died. I don't like that at all."

"I know, but it means we have to list Betsy as a suspect for now. Even if we don't believe it to be true, someone else could have used what she gave him," Ava said, making a slide with what I thought Ralph said to me then another slide with a list of suspects. Betsy was number one on the list.

"Well, if we are listing our friends, list Zed and Zander Zimmerman. Mick and I saw them and Ralph in an argument by the B&B last week, and then the brothers were with Ralph when Betsy brought the samples of her dessert. They weren't yelling, but there looked to be tension still. We may want to look into what that was all about," I said, noticing I was flattening a spot on the carpet with my strides.

"I know there is no connection that we have in front of us, but I'm listing Nestle. He's been up to something, we just don't know what. It wouldn't surprise me at all if he's somehow connected," Ava said, grabbing a picture of him, placing it in the slide, and typing furiously noting all the things she hated about him.

"Good point. For that matter, make a note that Mayor Cardinal and his assistant Tonya were talking near Ralph, plus there was a young man with them that I didn't recognize. Betsy was talking to him, so we can ask her who he was. Again, nothing to make them suspects, but they were in the area when it all went down," I said, finally sitting down.

"I'm making a list of people who have means, motive, and opportunity, and then another list where there are no connections yet who could be possible suspects." Ava turned to look at me. "I know you won't like this, but I'm adding Peggy and Stella to the possible suspect list. It's always the wife or significant other, and Stella was his part-time help and worked for Peggy some too—if nothing else, they should be able to offer us some information along the way."

"Eek, you're right, I don't like it at all. Maybe list them under the 'possible' list but put a note to go to them when we need more information," I said.

"Got it," Ava turned back to the computer.

"While we are here, can we start a new I-Spy Slide folder. Or, maybe two. One for who is the father of Lydia's baby. She named him Monty, and that is Mick's great-grandfather's name. Maya, Mick's mom, seems thrilled with Lydia and the baby," I said, fidgeting and finding myself pacing again. There were too many things running through my mind.

"I wouldn't give one worry about what his parents think. He doesn't seem to care, and he's told you his family is involved with the mafia. He broke away from them and changed his name," Ava encouraged me. As much as she made me batty at times, she was the best friend a girl could ask for.

"Easier said than done," I said, stopping in my tracks while holding up my index finger. "Hey, you mentioned Nestle. Let's start a slide for all the crimes that have taken place in Leavensport, starting with Ellie Siler. Then, let's list what we know about Nestle, like his ex-wife testifying against him and then going into witness protection and all the mafia connections—from Mick's family to Nestle to the Dominican Republic. There's something big happening. I can feel it. It's time we dig into it."

"You realize to do that legally—" Ava started.

"Yep, I'll start filling out the paperwork and studying for the PI exam. You get to ask Tabitha for me, though." I grinned, knowing that she was more than willing.

"Are you serious?" Ava nearly jumped out of the chair in joy and mouthed Y-E-S while using her fist to pound the air above her head, "in the meantime, they are opening the festival back up later today for the last day. We need to be there to find out some things."

"Okay, so we are tearing down the booth and closing out the till tonight after Carlos and Magda work the booth, then they are prepping for opening tomorrow," I said to Ava as we walked by the pizza booth where I saw Ralph take his last breath. I shivered and felt a pang of pain move through me.

"Yeah, and don't forget that we need to give them a break later, too."

"Right, it looks like Stella is over there running the pizza booth." I was surprised to see it open after everything that had happened and they moved it down a few spots between Delilah's craft corner and the Moore's dance studio booth.

"Hey, ladies," Stella said. Her eyes were puffy and her make-up was smudged.

"We were surprised to see you had the booth open after what happened to Ralph," I said.

"His entire life was that business. He would have wanted me to keep it going, and I plan to honor him," she said, brushing her dark bangs away from her face.

"That's real dedication. He was fortunate to have an employee like you," I said as Ava nodded in agreement.

"Had you witnessed Ralph having arguments with anyone recently?" Ava asked.

"You know he was from New York City. That's why he made the best New York-style pizza around. He had what he said was the secret to make the dough just right. I know that his business was booming and he was talking about purchasing some land and opening a second store. He asked me if I'd be interested in managing it," Stella said as tears sprang to her eyes.

"Any idea who he'd leave his store to if he died?" Ava asked.

"No, but I was contacted by an attorney who said I am to show up when his will is read, which seems strange to me," Stella shrugged her shoulders.

"That is interesting," Ava mumbled.

A group of people had formed around us. I noticed off to the side, people were putting things on the ground as a memorial to Ralph. Both people from Tri-City and Leavensport were adding to it.

One man snapped at Ava, "I'm not sure why you townies are here asking questions or leaving things for Ralph when it sounds like one of your own killed him!"

Ava's eyes blazed. "Excuse me. Do I even know you? I happen to be a licensed PI on this case, so I'd inform you to back way off, mister!"

"Who do you think you are talking to her that way?" Maria said, pushing through the crowd, coming to Ava's defense.

Delilah had been walking toward them and, judging from her expression, overheard the entire interaction.

Tension began to mount as the blend of mourners at Ralph's memorial began to fall into ranks of Leavensport residents versus Tri-City residents. I wasn't sure who was yelling at whom, nor did I think some of them knew either. It was all very jarring.

"Do I know you?" Delilah stepped in front of Maria, ignoring the rumbling feud going on.

"I'm Maria Milano. And who are you?" Maria straightened her shoulders and lifted her chin.

"I'm Delilah, Ava's girlfriend," she said with a smirk, reaching her hand out in all politeness.

Okay, this was all getting out of control. "Hello, everyone, quiet, please. HELLO!" I yelled at the crowd.

Someone in the crowd emitted an ear-splitting whistle, the kind you have to stick your fingers in your mouth to do—something I could never master. I turned to see Mick using his walker, standing behind me with his mother, Maya, next to him. The crowd was startled into silence.

"Folks, what you are all doing here is generous—that is leaving something in Ralph's memory. What's not so generous is standing and causing a scene and arguing. I'm sure he wouldn't want that happening on his behalf," Mick stated.

"It's true, he was a good man and would not want this," Tonya Morrison said.

Ava and I looked at each other, confused. Peggy had walked up and looked equally confused by Tonya's statement.

The crowd began to disperse amid angry grumbles.

I turned to Mick and smiled gratefully. His mother glared at me, and Mick acted as if he didn't see me. He turned around, and, using his walker, stomped off.

Ava had witnessed everything and seemed uncomfortable with Maria and Delilah as well. The two of them had scattered with the crowd. "Come on, let's go give Carlos and Magda a break. It will do us some good to focus on work," Ava said.

We went to Cast Iron Creations' booth and took over for an hour during the late afternoon rush. It was nice not to have to think about anything but gathering food and prepping. I found myself getting into a groove as I always did when working, and felt the weight of the world leave my shoulders for a little while.

A while later, I turned and saw that my Uncle Eddie and Uncle Wylie were walking our way. They seemed to be arguing. I wondered if it had something to do with the city versus the town folks. I hoped not. We don't need a feud going on.

"Hey guys, I'll make a couple of to-go boxes for you," I said, smiling, as Uncle Wylie nodded angrily toward me. That was weird. He was always so happy. I scooped out Carlos Mexican pot pies from the Dutch cast oven pot into two boxes and added a chunk of the jalapeno cheddar cornbread to each box and passed it to Ava to give to them.

"Um, Jolie, I think there is a problem here," Ava said, pointing to my uncles after I had handed the boxes of food to them.

"This is not the place to have this discussion," Uncle Eddie's mouth tightened as his body stiffened up.

"I don't see Shelly around here to tell you what to do," Uncle Wylie seethed, then suddenly opened the lid of the box and tossed the contents at his brother, who in turn, threw his food at Uncle Wylie.

Dark mole gravy and seasonings dripped to the to the ground, and I saw specks of yellow corn sliding down Uncle Wylie's face. All of that hard work wasted on some stupid family argument.

"Whoa, STOP!" I yelled. "A lot of work went into preparing that food! Now, stop making a spectacle of our family—people already think we're nuts as it is."

Both brothers' faces were contorted with anger.

What on earth was happening in this town?

Chapter Seven

I found out later that Grandma Opal, Tom Costello, my mom, Aunt Fern, and Mayor Nalini had all intervened with the two uncles yesterday afternoon at various spots around the festival. None of them could figure out what the two men were fighting about (or no one willing to admit it to me.)

While I had always looked forward to and enjoyed the previous Labor Day festivals, I'm not so sure I'll feel the same in future years if they all resembled this one.

Ava and I wanted to try and speak to Betsy yesterday, but the day got away from us, and before we knew what was happening, it was time to tear the booth down, store everything, and help to clean up around town. That continued into this morning because of so much chaos during the festival. We were working in the Leavensport Circle area, as it was the hot spot for the festival and had the most litter.

Since Carlos and Magda were already working that afternoon, we didn't ask them to cover us. Instead, we put a note up that we would open a few hours later than usual due to clean up after the festival.

"Are you okay?" I heard the concern in Ava's voice and turned quickly to see she was calling out to Betsy, who was walking out of the police station looking like a zombie.

"I-I-I," Betsy stammered.

"Come, sit," I said, leading her to a bench.

"Betsy, what happened?" Ava asked.

"Teddy said my s'more dessert killed him." Betsy's hazel eyes darted back and forth, filling with tears. She began to tremble and suddenly bent over to dry heave. Then she burst out in tears.

Ava and I gave her time to let it all out consoling her before Ava asked, "Teddy knows you didn't do this, right? Or else you wouldn't be out here now."

"He said they are early in the investigation. Ralph was poisoned, but Teddy wouldn't tell me any more than that. Then he advised me to get an attorney."

"He's making sure your interests are protected, Betsy," Ava said. "He has to do his job, but he didn't have to tell you that."

"You need to call Niko Mercurio today and fill him in on everything," I said. "Betsy, I know Teddy is your friend and we all grew up together but you shouldn't have spoken to him freely without an attorney present."

"She's right, call him and go over there now. Don't talk to the police again without him," Ava said.

"But I didn't do anything wrong," she pleaded.

"Honey, no one, including Teddy, thinks you did. It's just that it sounds like the evidence is pointing to you, and you need to be protected. Someone could be setting you up," I said, rubbing her back.

"Do you want us to go with you?" Ava asked.

"No, I've got my cell, and I'm going to walk. I could use the air," Betsy said, dragging herself off the bench, shoulders slumped.

"We need to figure out what poison was used," I told Ava as Betsy trudged away.

"I'll try to find out. I've been trying to make some contacts for things like this," Ava said, grabbing her phone to text.

"Who?" I asked.

"That's something you shouldn't know right now. Be sure to get going on getting your license."

I didn't like the sound of that.

We were finishing up, exhausted, but ready to head to work to open up when Stella came running up behind us in a tizzy.

"What's up, lady?" Ava asked. "Catch your breath!"

Stella had her hair in a ponytail today with wisps from her layers framing her face. Her make-up looked fabulous. She had a natural knack for doing her make-up perfectly, and I'd asked her if she would help me figure out if I had a spring, summer, or winter skin tone and the best coloring for my skin. Stella was born male, but she had always identified as a female. When Ava and I met her last November, she was in the process of fully transitioning. It's been so much fun having her help me with make-up and figuring out a style of clothes. We met up last Christmas while she worked part-time at a make-up counter, and she got me hooked on all things Urban Decay, which I'm told young people like.

"Sorry, I just had—" deep breath in, "to—" long exhale, "catch—you—both. This—" Stella was pointing to a gym bag that said "Ralph's New York Style Pizza Shop" with the Tri-City high school mascot, a mammoth, on it.

"What's in the bag?" I asked.

Stella stopped and took a few deep breaths, then unzipped the bag and held it open.

Ava and I gaped at each other as our mouths fell open.

"Is that—"

"NO! Not mine. After everything happened with Ralph, I went back to the city to put the money away, and in the safe was this. It wasn't there before the festival. He trusted me with the safe combination."

"How much is there?" Ava asked.

"They're hundred-dollar bills grouped by one-thousand dollars a strap and there are twenty-five of them. *Twenty-five thousand dollars*," Stella whispered. "I don't know what to do with it or where it came from. I found it at Ralph's shop in the back in his locker when I was cleaning it out. "

"Listen, Peggy hired us to investigate this. If you're comfortable with us taking it, then we can discuss it," Ava said.

"There's nothing to discuss! We have to give this to Teddy. It could help him figure out who killed Ralph." I gave Ava the duh look.

"I want to find out what happened to him, and I'm not comfortable holding onto this or having it in his pizza shop either. So, yeah, you take it." Stella readily handed it to me.

"I'll get it to him, but he's going to want to interview you about where you found it and if you touched all of the money. I put the gym bag over my shoulder and headed to the restaurant to drop off some things from the booth. Ava was in the car with me, chomping hard on gum.

"Could you close your mouth when you chew, please?"

"I'm nervous. This helps me think," she said, chewing harder.

"Well, it's not helping me. Where did that money come from? I guess it could all be legit," I said, pulling into the front of our restaurant on the street.

"Really, he's poisoned, then all of a sudden, twenty-five thousand shows up the weekend he is killed?"

"Yeah, good point," I said, getting out of the car with the bag. I planned on holding onto this until I got it to Teddy, which was going to be in a few minutes.

"I'll take all of the restaurant equipment and supplies out of the trunk and sit it by the door. You take that to Teddy. First, let me take some pictures of the bag inside and out and some close-ups of each bundle of money and some close-ups of the serial numbers on some of the bills," Ava said, reaching for her phone.

"Whoa, you are getting really smart about all this PI stuff," I said, watching her make sure each picture gave her the details she wanted to see.

"Got it, we'll add these to the slides later. Here, you take this to Teddy, and I'll get moving on opening up."

"Okay, Carlos and Magda prepped a lot last night, so not much to do," I said, waving and taking off toward the middle of town again. It was a lovely day, and I would have walked except I didn't want to chance anything with this much money.

It only took a couple of minutes to get there. I had to park further down the street because the courthouse and police station were near the mall. I grabbed my tote and the gym bag and headed for the police station. I saw Mick in his wheelchair coming out and wondered if he had a change of heart in coming back to work with Teddy. I thought I'd ask—

I felt my body jerk hard as it hit the ground. I shook my head in confusion and looked as someone with a ski mask, hoodie, and gloves ripped the gym bag from me and took off sprinting. It all happened so fast.

A few passersby had stopped to see if I was okay. Mick had rolled his wheelchair up.

"Jolie, are you okay?" He looked serious. He pulled out his phone and dialed, speaking into it in low tones for a moment. Seconds later, Keith pulled out of the police lot in a cruiser.

"I'm fine, but—" I thought about the gym bag full of money gone.

"Who was that? What did they take?" Mick asked. "Keith will drive around and see if he spots anyone suspicious, but I'm guessing whoever it was has already ducked into hiding."

"Um, I need to see Teddy. Are you back working for him? Is that why you're here?"

"Wow, you are like Tabitha. Answer a question with a question," he grinned.

"Well, I hope you are taking care of yourself. You are not supposed to be using that if you don't have to. The last two times I've seen you, you've been in it," I crossed my arms.

"That's because I'm taking care of him," Maya came strolling out, dripping in diamonds. She had what looked to be several carats on her ring finger.

"Have you talked to his doctor? This is not helping him," I said, not caring if she liked me or not.

"I don't need to speak to his doctor. I'm his mother. I know what's best for him."

"That obviously isn't true," I said, staring her down. "You are doing the infusion this week, right?" I looked at Mick, concerned.

"I'm not sure." He looked at the ground.

"Let's get out of here," Maya said, pushing him away.

I grumbled out loud and yelled, "UGH! THAT WOMAN!" as several startled people jumped back away from me. I headed in to Teddy to report everything that had happened.

"Where have you been?" Ava yelled from the kitchen as I came dragging myself into work.

"I'm sorry, I should have called."

"Never mind, you need to help me get caught up on these orders," she said, running from kitchen to the front, delivering one meal to one table and another to another table while people sat watching their partners eat with nothing in front of them.

"One table at a time," I seethed.

"Do NOT tell me how to do a job for two when you are off lollygagging around," Ava spit out.

I went back and got busy putting the eight orders together that sat in front of my face.

Forty minutes later, it slowed down, and Ava and I sat to have a Coke.

Ava took the glass I handed her, giving me a hostile look.

"Look, before you say anything, someone stole the bag of money right as I was trying to walk it into Teddy. Mick was there in his wheelchair but couldn't do anything. Then, I went in to report it all to Teddy. That's why I was late."

"Wait, what? Someone stole the money? How on earth did you manage that?"

"Oh, I was walking into the police station, and a person with a ski mask and hoodie looked like they could use a cool twenty-five grand, so I just handed it over," I sneered.

"You aren't funny. Did you see who took it?"

"I only saw the ski mask and the hoodie. Oh, and I'm fine, thanks for asking," I said, narrowing my eyes at her.

"I didn't ask because you showed up and kicked butt getting the orders out, Jolie, so obviously you are fine. If you are going to be a PI like me, then you have to get used to getting roughed up a bit here and there!"

"What? I HAVE to get used to it like YOU? When have you been attacked? I've been attacked on multiple occasions. It's like I have a huge sign on my head, begging for jerks to attack me. YOU have never been assaulted!"

"We don't need to quibble over minute details," Ava said as Mrs. Seevers came bouncing in.

"Girls, have you heard the latest?" Mrs. Seevers eyes twinkled. She was *so* hoping we hadn't heard and she could be the ones to tell us.

"No, what's new?" Ava asked.

"A lot! Seems like that cute girl that worked for that pizza guy, she went missing."

"Stella?!?" Ava and I yelled at once.

"Yes, that's right. Teddy is all in an uproar, thinking she may be the main suspect. I guess Ralph left his pizza empire to her, and all his earthly possessions."

Ava and I looked at each other perplexed.

"That's not the craziest thing to happen," Mrs. Seevers was practically drooling.

"What more could there be?" I asked.

"Lydia is *related* to Jackson Nestle!"

My mind was like a working machine that had a wrench shoved into it. I froze in horror.

Chapter Eight

That night, Ava brought her girls to my place so the kittens could play with my four. Seven cats in one house was a tad overwhelming, especially when three were babies with a lot of energy.

"Okay, so Stella. I added her to the suspect list, but I also want to add her to a victim slide. We don't know if she took off or something happened to her," Ava said.

"I know, I've tried her cell phone twenty times today and only get voicemail. I tried texting, calling Ralph's store, calling Peggy to see if she heard anything," I said.

"Did she know about Ralph leaving everything to Stella?" Ava whipped her head around.

I grabbed my Monet Impressionism large pillow and pulled it to me on the couch. "No. Well, kind of." I threw the pillow back on the sofa and stood to pace.

"What does that mean?"

"She didn't know what was in his will. She said she didn't expect to be in it because they only recently started dating. She said that Ralph was pleased with Stella when she started working for him. I guess she told him about the transition and he started acting differently."

"Ugh, just what Stella needed. She was already vulnerable as it was," Ava wrinkled her nose.

"Yeah, but Ralph obviously got over it. Stella continued to work for him, and he left everything to her. It would be great if we could talk to her about it."

"You're sure Stella isn't the one who took the money from you, right?" Ava was typing notes on a slide.

"Of course I'm sure. She would never do that! Besides, she couldn't get rid of that bag quick enough!"

"Okay, I had to ask," Ava stopped typing and turned to look at me.

Just then, my phone rang, interrupting us. My brow furrowed. "It's one of my cousins."

"Hello?"

"Hey, Jolie, all five of us are on speaker," Tink said.

"Oh, hey, guys! Ava's here, can I put you on speaker?"

"Sure!" I heard Serenity yell out, probably from behind wherever Tink was.

I put them on speaker, letting Ava know it was all of them.

"Hey, Tucker crew," Ava bellowed.

"What up . . . hey girl . . . what's going on?" Multiple voices rang out on the other end of the phone simultaneously.

"Ummm," Tink started nervously, "we were wondering if either of you know what is going on with our dad and Uncle Wylie?"

Ava and I looked at each other.

"I was hoping one of you could shed some light on all of this for me," I said, shrugging my shoulders at Ava, who returned the gesture.

"We have no clue," Kevin spoke up. "But I'm guessing Aunt Fern and Aunt Patty and Grandma Opal all know."

"You think?" I asked.

"There's something going on from way back that they all know. They aren't sharing," Sadie said.

"I agree," I said.

"Did any of you ask your mom or dad?" Ava asked.

"I did," Tink said while laughing his airy laugh. "They gave me the death glare."

"I hate it when parents do that," I said, crossing my arms.

"Will you see what you can find out?" Karly asked, pleading with us.

I looked at Ava, who nodded.

"We'll try." We hung up.

"Family," Ava said.

"Hashtag truth. One mystery at a time—back to where we were. Make a slide for motive, means, and opportunity," I said.

"Whoa, someone is getting serious about this," Ava laughed.

"I got my paperwork together, filled out the application, found online courses, and signed up. So, I'm moving forward. But it will take some time."

"I see you are taking the basic course on what we always look for," Ava chuckled.

"Yep, so, motive first," I held up five fingers and counted off, "One, that money could easily be a motive, but first we have to figure out where it came from. Two—"

"The Zimmermans. We need to find out what that argument was over. Could be motive," Ava said while typing it into a slide.

"Right. Three, the poison. Teddy said it came from Betsy's dessert. We need to talk to her and ask if she made those samples and if anyone could have had access to them."

"Oh yeah, I found out from my source that it was strychnine poison."

"Who is the source?"

"Anonymous," Ava said. "Now, strychnine is toxic, odorless, but it has a bitter taste. I looked it up earlier and made some notes."

"Hang on." I reached for my phone and texted Betsy. My phone dinged a few minutes later as I was telling Ava my thoughts. "Yep, she said it was dark chocolate she used in her s'mores dessert, so that would hide the bitterness."

"Good call! You will make a great PI one day!"

"Thanks," I held my shoulders back and lifted my chin.

"That's the means if what Teddy said is right. The dessert. Now, who had the opportunity. We need to see if we can meet with Betsy tomorrow," Ava said.

"The Zimmermans were there when Betsy took the dessert to him. The question is, did he eat it all immediately, sit it down and come back to it? Was it meant for a Zimmerman brother and not Ralph?" I held my hands up in the air.

"All good points." Ava typed, then turned in the swivel chair. "Man, if it was meant for one of them instead. That makes everything more complicated."

"No one said PI work would be easy."

"I'm going to text Betsy asking if we can meet with her tomorrow to talk to her," Ava said, reaching for her cell.

I had the next day off of work to run some errands. The first thing I did before leaving was to call Dr. Delagada's office and left a message for her with her receptionist.

"Right. T-u-c-k-e-r," I spelled it out for the third time.

"So, F-u"

"NO! T. T as in Tom."

"Oh, sorry! Okay, what is the message?"

What was the message? "Well, could you tell her that Mick Meiser, who is her patient, he's supposed to start a new medicine this week for his MS. It's an infusion. Also, he's not supposed to use his wheelchair, but he is. I don't think he's taking his Lexipro because he seems depressed. But I think she said it could take some time to get into his system. And his mother, she is encouraging him to stay in his wheelchair because it makes her feel better about the horrific mother she was his entire life. It's like she's keeping him prisoner or something. Plus, I don't know if he is going to therapy. That's something else that Dr. Delagada told him to do. And he's barely talking to me now, so how am I supposed to find out? I mean, I'm worried about him. I need you to tell Dr. Delagada all of this."

Dead silence.

"Um, could you repeat that and go slower, please? Oh wait, can I put you on hold?"

"NO! Can I get her voicemail, please?"

"I'm sorry, ma'am, she prefers we write her messages down. One moment, please."

I waited more than a minute then hung up. That was fine, I had an appointment with Tabitha, and I'd snoop around or blatantly ask her.

I headed over to Kwani's filling station to fill up my gas tank before I went to the grocery store. I finished and headed inside to grab a blend of cherry and blueberry slushy to take with me on my trip.

I turned to see Mayor Cardinal's assistant Tonya with that young man from the other day. "Hi, Tonya, nice to see you again."

Tonya looked at me for a long moment and scratched her temple.

"It's Jolie. Jolie Tucker. I had to meet with Mayor Cardinal a while back—"

"Oh my goodness gracious, yes. I'm so sorry, dear. My mind—I'll tell you what—don't get older!" She looked at the young man and laughed. He put his hands in his pocket and rocked back on his heels. "Oh, sorry, this is my son, Elijah. He's getting ready to start his second year of college at Tri-City, but he's been helping our mayor out lately for a little pocket cash."

Elijah took one hand out of his pocket and reached to shake mine. I had also grabbed a king-sized Snickers bar and a bag of barbeque chips, so I had to juggle those with my slushy to shake his hand. He was one of those guys that still wore his class ring, and he was also wearing his high school letter jacket.

"Hi, I'm running some errands and gathering the essentials." I felt my face blush at what a pig I must have looked like right then.

"I hear you! We were here for the festival, and my car broke down. So, we stayed at that lovely B&B last night while my car is getting fixed by that helpful man over at the We Care shop. I wish the city had some cute titles like that for some of our shops," Tonya cooed.

"I'll talk to John about it," Elijah burst out eagerly. "You know we're working to make things more small-town friendly with—"

Tonya interrupted him, "Well, it's about time for us to go check on that car. Let's go, son."

She nearly shoved him out the door. Now what was all of that about?

I ran my errands and was putting everything away when the phone rang. I saw it was Lydia. I had to admit, Ava and I were both curious about the whole Nestle thing. I was more curious about the name of her baby.

"Hey, Lydia," I said, putting the cell on speaker while putting the rest of my groceries away.

"Hi," she whispered. "Hold on."

Okay, I thought, *you called me!*

"Sorry about that. I was putting Monty down for a nap."

"How are you and the baby doing? I haven't had a chance to visit," I said, wondering if I'd even thought about a visit yet.

"We're okay. There's a lot going on in our little hamlet right now."

"Um, not to be too upfront, but Mrs. Seevers is spreading rumors that you are related to Nestle."

More silence.

"That's true, unfortunately. I never knew it, though, but I guess he's known all along."

She did not sound happy at all. It kind of made me feel bad for her for a moment.

"You know my dad's in jail. I've never had any sort of a relationship with him, and my mom is pretty worthless all around as moms go."

Okay, now I felt like a brat again. "You haven't had the best family life. It's amazing how well you've turned out."

Lydia let out a loud laugh, "Oh man, that had to be difficult for you to say."

I grinned to myself.

"Good ole dad's family is from Canada. So, Uncle Jackson."

"But the last name," I said.

"Dad changed his name when he moved here. I never knew that, either. Mom told me all about it at the festival, not long before...well, you know, Monty decided to join us. I guess Nestle has been sniffing around my mom, and she knew everything this entire time. I still don't think I know the entire story, and to be honest, I'm not sure I want to know."

"Whoa." I stopped in my tracks before sitting the box of Cheerios on the shelf.

"Exactly. Anyway, not why I'm calling. What is going on with Mick?"

"Um, I'm guessing you know more than I do, and if so, you tell me!"

"His mother is a piece of work," Lydia said.

"Really? She seems in love with you and that child. She's just beside herself that you've named the child after Mick's great grandfather," I said, hoping she'd tell me why.

"All I know is that he is miserable. He's acting like a victim, which is annoying. Maya may tell you she likes me, but she isn't friendly to me either. She seems to want to get Mick away from the baby as fast as possible. I think she likes to play games."

"Uh, you used to be that way too," I couldn't help saying.

"I did used to be like that. I think I've grown up a lot in a few short months. I'd like to think little Monty helped me with that."

"Why 'Monty?'" I blurted out.

"Trust me, Jolie, you don't want me to name this child after the father."

Chapter Nine

I had lots of plans to catch up on errands and cleaning on my day off. I did get some things accomplished. The first thing I did was to call Gemma to inquire about Peggy and ask if there was any news on Stella. No one had heard anything yet, and Peggy was still beside herself. I only had spoiled milk in the refrigerator, so going to the store took quite a long time to fill up the fridge and cabinets again—nothing worse than a chef with an empty kitchen. After talking to Lydia and the events of the last few days, a long, loungy nap sounded blissful.

BRRIIINNGGGG-BRRIIINNGGGG! I'd been sleeping soundly for over an hour when I heard my doorbell ringing over and over and over again. I jolted awake, thinking it was my cell and grabbed it from the nightstand. "Hello?" I grumbled. No one there. BRRIIIINNNNNGGGGG! I sat up, shaking the cobwebs out of my head, then realizing it was the doorbell still going off.

"Good Lord," I said to my four kitties who were scrambling under my feet, also wondering what that annoying noise that awoke them was.

"What?!" I opened the door with crazy eyes.

"You really shouldn't come to the door with wild eyes when your hair is insane like that,"

Grandma Opal said, pushing past me with Aunt Fern and my mom, Patty, trotting behind her.

"Is there an emergency of some kind? Who was ringing the doorbell like a woodpecker at his favorite tree?"

"There is a family emergency," Grandma said, fanning her face.

"What's going on?" I said, noting that my mom and Aunt Fern were rolling their eyes. "I guess not a huge emergency."

"Your uncles are at each other's throats, and we'd like you and Ava to find out what exactly is going on."

"Grandma, maybe we should all stay out of it," I said, turning on the kettle.

"You were the one who wanted them back in our lives. So, here they are. Now, figure out what is going on!"

"Are you planning to pay us?" I asked, grabbing some cups from the cupboard.

"Pay you? We're family. Family doesn't pay," Grandma declared.

"Oh yes, family pays when they are asking someone who owns a business, works part-time helping her BFF with her PI business, and is juggling multiple things—yes, we will look into it for a fee. I will ask Ava about a family discount, but that is up to her. That's the best offer you're going to get," I said, eyeballing Grandma, who was holding her stare like a cowboy in a stand-off, waiting to draw.

"Oh, okay, fine. I want to know what's going on—but you remind Ava that I helped raise her!"

"Grandma, have you thought about just asking either one of them what is going on?" I looked at my mom like how she could not realize how easy that was.

Grandma's lips thinned as she harrumphed, "I did. They won't tell me."

I sighed, made the tea for everyone, and changed the subject.

Ava came over after her shift at the restaurant.

"So, my grandma wants to know what's up with my uncles' feud. I told her she has to pay us to find out."

"Why doesn't she just ask?"

"That's what I said. She did."

"They don't want nosey pants to know their business, aye?"

"Smart men."

"You are going to make your family pay us?"

"Yeah, I told them I'd ask you if you'd give them a discount. Grandma told me to remind you she helped raise you."

Ava laughed, "I'll give them a seventy-five percent discount."

"Too generous," I said, stuffing my face with Carlos's enchiladas that Ava brought for us and talking with a mouthful. "Make it only twenty percent. We don't want them coming to us left and right."

"Hashtag truth," Ava said, also around a mouthful.

"Man, he is going to do a killing at his new restaurant," I said, shaking my head.

"I know. His food is so good."

We inhaled the rest of the enchiladas. "I know this is weird, but I'm craving chips and salsa. I can whip up some homemade salsa real quick for a snack before we start on the slides.

"Not weird, if we were at his future restaurant we would have had that as an appetizer. I see you finally went to the store."

"Yeah, I spent a ton of money to restock. I can't believe it's been close to three weeks since I went." I usually went to the store almost daily for fresh ingredients for the restaurant and I'd grab things for home while there. Even though I cooked all day for a living, I loved cooking and baking at home too. Things had been so nuts lately, I'd been only buying for the restaurant and bringing food home from there to eat.

"I'll start yet another file for your family while you make the salsa."

"Geesh, we'll have to hire more help at the restaurant if we keep picking up PI business or start saying no," I said, grabbing the lime juice, garlic, cilantro, Herdez medium salsa, cumin, and chipotle powder.

"So, Betsy came into the restaurant today," Ava said as I got the food processor out and added all the ingredients. "You're making that thin, right?"

"I like it thin and juicier too! What did she say?"

"She made a huge tray of samples from what she was selling, and when she had a lull, she'd walk nearby and offer them to people to try. She said no one helped her make the desserts, but once she gave them out to people, she had no way of knowing what happened."

She stopped talking when I turned the processor on to blend and thin our semi-homemade salsa. I poured the salsa into cute little cast-iron bowls I bought for things like this and grabbed a bag of tortilla chips, a basket and put a checkered cloth inside, poured in a bunch of chips, shoved all the dirty food processor parts in the sink, running water on them for easier clean up later. I took our snack through the corridor from the kitchen to the living room, where Ava had her laptop set up on the coffee table.

"Try it," I said, going back for a couple of cans of Coke Zero.

"Perfect," Ava said through crunches.

"Oy, okay, so, we have a file that we're working on for Peggy about what happened to Ralph. You just added a file about my cray-cray family. Now, Lydia called me earlier, telling me to trust her that I didn't want her to name that baby after the father. What could that possibly mean?"

"You don't think she and Nestle did the nasty before they knew they were related, do you? Remember, we saw them arguing a while back." Ava's face scrunched up as if she'd smelled something horrid.

"EWWWWW! No, do not even go there. Plus, while Lydia is not my all-time favorite person, even she wouldn't stoop so low to entertain Nestle. She was less than thrilled to find out she's related to him."

Ava held her hands up, "Okay, okay, I mean, who could it be? Why is it such a secret?"

"What?" I asked, knowing that concerned look on Ava's face.

"I mean, she named it after Mick's great-grandfather. You said his mother is in love with her. He offered to be her Lamaze coach. Would they out and out lie to your face?" Ava looked like she regretted asking the moment it left her mouth.

"I don't want to believe that," I said hesitantly. "I do have to admit that it had crossed my mind, though."

"I shouldn't have said it. Thinking about it now, you and he were an item most of the time she was pregnant. She called you after every class. She's been trying to be friendlier. I don't think both of them could pull off that kind of lie and keep it going."

"I know, I agree. I'm not thrilled with Mick now, but I can't believe he'd do that to me. Plus, Lydia said his mom hates her too. She's just playing games with me."

"That's good," Ava said, making a few notes in the Lydia file. "We'll figure out who the dad is."

I laughed at Ava enjoying Maya hating someone besides just me.

"Back to your family. Have *you* thought about asking your uncles what is up? They may be more willing to tell you than Grandma."

"Let me call Uncle Eddie right now," I said, grabbing my landline.

"You know you are the only person in town to still have a landline, right? Even the Seevers don't use them anymore," Ava scoffed.

"I don't care what other people do," I said, cradling the phone to my ear.

"Hello," I heard Uncle Eddie's wife, Shelly, say.

"Hey, Aunt Shelly, this is Jolie. Is Uncle Eddie there?"

"Nope, he's out and about, what's up with you?"

"Not much. Hey, do you know what is going on between Uncle Wylie and Uncle Eddie?"

"Why do you and everyone else in your family assume I am the one who knows what is going on? It's offensive! I haven't done anything!"

"Um, okay, I just thought maybe Uncle Eddie said something to you," I said, eyes wide, staring at Ava and shrugging my shoulders.

"Well, he didn't. I have to go." *Click.* The line went dead.

"Wow, so she was not thrilled with my question."

"What's her problem?"

"Make a note that she's crazy too. I'm assuming my family has been nosing around, but she was quick to claim her innocence when I wasn't even blaming her for anything."

"I'm noting that. That is suspicious. How well do you know her?"

"Not well at all. Calling Uncle Wylie now."

"Hello," Uncle Wylie sounded jovial as usual.

"Hey, Uncle Wylie, it's Jolie."

He laughed his airy chuckle, "Yeah, you are the only person who shows up on my caller ID as a private caller. Calling from the landline, huh?"

"Not you too!" I rolled my eyes.

"What's ya need?"

"Um, are you and Uncle Eddie okay? I know he and Grandma have their issues, but I didn't think you two were at odds," I rushed through the words before he could object.

"Not a lot to say on that matter," he said.

"It's just that they're all back in our lives now, and I don't understand why there has to be so much animosity. Are you taking Grandma's side from way back whenever there was bad blood before?"

"I'm not that thrilled with your grandmother right now, either. But I'll keep my mouth shut. I have to go." Another click and dead line.

"Wow." I repeated it all to Ava.

"No one is making it easy to figure anything out," Ava said.

"Why is Grandma hiring us to figure out something that seems like she already knows the answer to?"

"It's your family. Anything is possible."

"That's true," I said. "I have an idea. Let's head over to talk to Betsy again."

As we were walking into Chocolate Capers, I noticed Betsy's front window display showed chocolate nursing shoes, construction boots, and ballet shoes. Betsy loved to do chocolate models of different things to display in her front window. This was one of the many new things she had done since taking over her Aunt Ellie's shop.

We walked in, and there wasn't a customer in sight. Betsy came from the back. "Hey, ladies. Need an afternoon pick-me-up?"

"Oh, we just ate a huge lunch," Ava said, rubbing her stomach.

Betsy nodded, and her shoulders drooped. I suddenly wondered if people were boycotting her shop with the rumors flying over her dessert poisoning Ralph.

"Actually, those chocolate-covered cake pops look wonderful," I said, looking for the smallest treat I could stuff into my overly full stomach.

Ava seemed to pick up on the cue. "Wow, they do look good. I'll take one too."

Typically, her display cases were half empty, and she was in the back, making more treats to add, but today everything was full.

The business phone rang, and Betsy stared at it.

"We aren't in a hurry," I said.

"Hello?" Betsy said, then said it three more times then hung up.

She grabbed the cake pops and went to wrap them. Her body was tense.

"Betsy, who was that?"

"People keep calling me and saying horrible things. I don't think it's anyone from here. I'm guessing it's some people from Tri-City. I had some not so pleasant things spray-painted on my garage when I woke up this morning."

"Did you make a police report?" Ava asked.

"Why would I do that? They think I'm guilty too."

Betsy looked like she was coming apart at the seams.

"No one here thinks you are guilty, Betsy. You need to let Teddy know what's going on," I said.

Betsy rang up our cake pops, took the money, handed them over then grabbed a napkin to wipe her eyes. "As if all of this isn't bad enough, I've got some man I don't even know calling saying I owe money on my loan. And I don't!"

"You have a loan? I thought your aunt left you this place?" Ava asked.

"I took out a loan to remodel, and Aunt Ellie still owed on some things. I took care of it all by consolidating it into one loan with the credit union."

"So, who is calling you?" I asked.

"I don't know. I've only worked with Keith's sister, Denise."

"It's only been a few days. Things will get back to normal. Our restaurant hasn't had as much business after the festival. You know how it is. Everyone goes there, splurges, then eats at home for a week or two," I said, trying to make her feel better.

"Meantime, I'm calling Teddy and having him come here. You need to report it. I'd suggest having Niko be here to be sure Teddy doesn't ask anything about Ralph," Ava said, pointing to Betsy's phone, signaling for her to call Niko.

"She's right. You need to protect yourself from all sides right now."

"Have you heard anything about Stella or how Peggy is doing?"

"I've been calling and texting Peggy. She's working. I imagine it helps her to do that. She hasn't heard anything from Stella. We all keep trying to call. Magda, who works for us, she's friends with Stella. I guess when Stella gets overwhelmed, she's been known to take off for up to a week at a time."

"I know, but with everything that happened, don't you think someone should report it? She worked for Ralph," Betsy said as Ava got off the phone.

"You can do that too when Teddy gets here. I told him what happened and why you didn't report it, about Stella when I heard you both talking, and I told him I am the one who recommended Niko be here. So, you don't have to worry about him thinking you're guilty."

Betsy let out a long exhale. "Thank you, both. I don't know what I'd do without you. Lydia has been calling me daily, too."

"You two on friendlier terms?" I asked. Betsy and Lydia had been best friends growing up. They ended up in nursing school together, then working together. When Betsy's Aunt Ellie was murdered, she left Chocolate Capers to her. Lydia had a lot of resentment when Betsy left nursing. Lydia wasn't thrilled that for a little while, I thought she had killed Ellie, either.

"I contacted her when I heard she was pregnant. We slowly talked more and began meeting for coffee. We aren't back where we used to be, but maybe someday."

"I need to run an errand. Are you okay if we take off?" Ava asked, looking at her watch.

"Oh, I'm fine. Thanks again." Betsy waved us off.

"Where are you in such a hurry to go?" asked Ava.

"The credit union. I hope Denise is working. I want to find out what's up."

Chocolate Capers wasn't too far from the credit union, so we decided to walk. They closed in fifteen minutes, but we still had plenty of time to get there.

Walking past Costello's grocery store, I saw Colleen, the town's coroner, huddled on her cell with her back to us. She seemed to be wanting privacy. I used the back of my hand to hit Ava's arm and pointed.

Ava got the cue and we tip-toed nearer to where she stood. Tom had a display of pumpkins near where she stood in the corner. I grabbed a basket in case we were caught snooping.

I started handling the pumpkins and looked up to see Ava go inside the store. What on earth was she doing?

Colleen had her index finger in her ear and wasn't whispering, but she wasn't talking loudly either. I took a few steps closer and picked up a small pumpkin and began using both hands to push either side to see how firm it was.

"At this point, I don't ... made ... his stomach or ... verison ... area. They all look to be ... measurements. There ... bruising as ..."

I was only hearing part of what Colleen was saying. She continued to talk but turned around. I panicked, and for some reason, tossed the small pumpkin high into the air.

"What are you doing?" Tom Costello asked.

He startled me, and I didn't catch it. It splattered all over the sidewalk as pumpkin goo flew on my pants and splattered Colleen's khakis and crisp, white shirt.

"Gotta go," she got off the phone as Ava came out with a small bag.

"Jolie, what on earth?" Ava asked.

"I'm sorry, I wanted to—um—buy a smaller pumpkin. I heard a rumor that if they are small, they can—um—go bad. So, I heard that tossing in the air and catching helped to know if—if—it's good or not," I stumbled along, making it up as I went. "I'm so sorry, Colleen. I can give you some money for dry cleaning."

"Don't worry about it. I've heard that too," Colleen said. She was always so quiet and well-kept. It seemed like nothing ever got to her. I guess that was a good way to be if you had to deal with dead people for a living.

Colleen walked off, unaffected.

"I feel bad," I said to Ava.

"I think having pumpkin brains splash all over her is the least of her worries based on her job," Ava said.

Tom nodded.

"Here's some money. I'm sorry," I said, digging into my tote.

"Ah, don't worry about it. We'll soon enough be family. Family shouldn't have to pay," Tom said, pointing at me. I wondered if Grandma told him about my charging her for the uncles. He scurried back into his store.

"Where did you go?" I asked Ava.

"The bathroom, then I bought a pack of gum and asked for a bag."

"Oh," I said, squinting my eyes.

"The bathrooms right there," Ava pointed to the wall where Colleen was standing. "There's a vent up there, and I opened it."

I looked up to see the flaps of the vent wide open.

"AHHH! I only caught bits and pieces of the conversation. Something about bruising," I said.

"On his stomach and his ribs. There were indentions around all the bruised areas. We'll have to make a note."

"You know the Zimmerman's have been known to get into a lot of fights over the years, and they were in a couple of heated arguments with him."

"Yeah, and Zed has that spiked leather jacket, and he wears those spiked gloves. He rode his motorcycle to the festival. I remember seeing him get off it. Those gloves always make me laugh." Ava shook her head, and long loose curls bounced around her face.

"Yeah, well, this would not be funny."

We finally walked into the small old brick building that housed the town's credit union a few minutes before they were closing. Luckily, Denise was there. Keith's sister was a little older than us, with short brown hair and shaggy bangs, and she loved me in spite of me breaking her brother's heart. I think she was holding out, believing that we would end up together eventually.

"Well, hey there, ladies. Long time no talk!" Denise declared.

She was always up for a chat, thank goodness. She could be one of those employees who watches the clock for closing time and glares at anyone coming in at the last minute. Kind of like Wanda over there, giving Ava and me the stink face. I smiled brightly and did a finger wave.

"We close in two minutes," Wanda called, gnawing on her gum, looking at us over her narrow glasses sitting low on her nose.

Ava looked at Wanda, rolled her eyes, and turned to Denise. "Quick question. Betsy is getting calls about her loan she took out here on the restaurant. Before you say anything, I understand you can't give out information. But do you know of a man that works here who would call anyone about a loan that was past due? Last I knew, it was all women who work here after Eric retired."

Denise's demeanor shifted from excited to chat to looking at her watch then looking over at Wanda. "You know, can we talk about this later. I forgot I have to get home to the kids as soon as possible. Football and marching band practice!" Denise took the volume of her voice down several notches, glancing sideways at Wanda to make sure the bank manager didn't hear.

"Denise, if you need to go outside to talk to your friends, I can count your drawer," Wanda said, walking toward the front door and turning the closed sign around.

"We won't keep her too long," Ava said, giving Denise a look.

"Well, come on, I need to lock up," Wanda said.

Denise looked torn but slumped her shoulders and followed us outside as Wanda locked the door behind us.

"What is going on?" I asked. "You know you can trust us if you're in some sort of trouble."

Denise rubbed the back of her neck, looked around nervously, and shook her head.

"Denise, tell us," Ava prompted.

"I could get fired. My kids—I can't." Denise looked around the street.

"Who are you afraid of?" I asked.

"Listen, I did do a loan for Betsy. I've been doing loans for different people—it's just—" tears welled up in her eyes with a look of fear.

"Maybe we should talk somewhere more private?" I asked, looking from Ava to Denise.

Denise perked up and turned to me. "Can I come to your place tomorrow night? Say, around nine p.m.?"

That seemed late for a visit, but I didn't want her to change her mind.

"Sure," I said, and Denise knocked for Wanda to let her back in.

"What on earth is going on now?" Ava asked.

"I don't know. Whatever it is—it's not good."

Chapter Ten

The next day, as we left at the end of our shift, I saw Gemma getting out of her car and walking toward the restaurant.

"Hi, Gemma. We're just getting off work for the day. Ava will be out in a bit. Where's Peggy?"

"She's home with Stella. I wanted to give the two of them some time together, and I wanted to fill you both in on the news since you are investigating Ralph's death," Gemma said.

"Wait, Stella is okay then? I need to call Teddy. I think Betsy reported her as a missing person," I said, digging through my tote for my phone.

"It's okay. Betsy phoned Peggy to tell her how sorry she was about Ralph. She was so worried about Peggy thinking she had something to do with it, and she was worried about Stella and told Peggy that she reported her missing. So, when Stella showed back up a few hours ago, I called Leavensport police station to let them know."

"Oh, okay. Where was Stella?"

"Like we thought, she took off. She was upset about Ralph—well—we thought she was overwhelmed by the murder and then him leaving everything to her. Turns out, it was more than that, and she needed some space to think everything through."

"What more could there possibly be?"

"Stella caught Ralph with Tonya Morrison in Tonya's car in the alley outside his pizza shop about a month ago," Gemma blurted out.

My eyes bugged out as Ava came out overhearing that last part.

"Excuse me, what?" Ava said a little too loudly.

I shook my head, confused. "Here, sit." I pulled out one of the gold-colored steel chairs from the matching tables we had put out front under the awning of our restaurant for pleasant spring, summer, and fall days.

Gemma repeated everything she had just told me while I worked to process it all.

"Tonya's married, though, right? Or is separated or divorced?"

"She's married with a kid in college. Stella is friends with her kid," Gemma said.

"So, Stella never told Peggy about it?" Ava asked.

"Not until today when she got back. Stella confronted Ralph about it after it happened, and he told her that Tonya's son was working with him on purchasing some land between here and Tri-City. Ralph told her he wanted to keep the purchase quiet until he was sure, but Elijah, Tonya's son, told his mom that Ralph seemed like he was on the fence about the purchase. So, Ralph said Tonya was trying to close the deal. That's what she saw and why she said it was nothing," Gemma shrugged her shoulders.

"Whoa, that's a lot of info. Did Stella believe him? Do you believe it?" Ava asked.

"I don't know what to think. All I know is my best friend is beside herself with the news, and she doesn't know what to think either."

"Well, I for one wouldn't put it past Tonya," I said, lowering my chin and leaning forward like a seasoned gossip. "I met her when I had a meeting with Mayor Cardinal. I overheard her talking about him while I was hiding in a bathroom stall. It sounded like they are more than co-workers. Then, I witnessed a strange interaction between the two of them when she took me to his office. He was all professional, but she seemed like she was making claims on *her* man. It wasn't too much stretch of the imagination that they were having an affair."

"Really?" Gemma said. "Well, that may make Peggy feel better about all of this."

"Obviously, I don't know much of anything about Ralph or Tonya, but it's all so strange."

"Did Stella tell either of you about the twenty-five grand she found in the gym bag at Ralph's shop?" I asked.

"I did," Ava said as Gemma nodded.

"I wonder if that money was connected to the land purchase? Like a down payment?" I asked.

"Now, that would make sense," Ava said. "We need to get back and make a lot of notes."

"Yep, one other thing," Gemma said. "There was a city assembly meeting. Mayor Cardinal is gung-ho on buying up all that land between Tri-City and Leavensport. Also, there's a bit of a ruckus because the area at the edge of the city, the first thing people would see as they come into Tri-City, is poverty-stricken and pretty run down. He is looking to buy up all the dilapidated buildings to redevelop the area from Leavensport to the city, moving into the center of the metropolis. His overall goal is gaining tourism, and I think he's planning to draw visitors in with Leavensport's small village charm, then pull them into the city for convenience and shopping. He's looking to fund a multi-million-dollar project along with working with the Small Business Development Center, Cultural Heritage Tourism Grant, and Ohio Grant Watch to fund a railway from Tri-City to Leavensport for—"

"Whoa, a railway? It's not that far just using the highway." Ava said.

"Right. He's getting a lot of pushback on this from citizens. He's determined to have a railway track with a vintage train to take people back and forth as part of a tourist attraction. He's got all kinds of statistics that support railways being more cost-effective. I have to admit the pictures he showed us of the vintage train were pretty cool. I hated that I loved the idea. You know, politics— hard to know what's for good and not-so-good purposes."

"Wow, something else for us to look into," Ava said, looking at me.

"Gemma, do you know where Ralph was going to buy the land?" I asked.

"No, I don't. Stella may know, though. I can ask her when I get back."

"Yeah, it may help us to know. Can you call or text if you find out?" I asked.

"Sure thing," she said, and headed back to her car, where she ran into Bradley.

Ava nudged me, and we watched them. He looked to be fidgeting and nervous around her. Gemma seemed to be blushing. They were so cute, reminding me of two teens who liked each other. Then, Lahiri came up behind him. We could tell by their body language he was introducing them awkwardly. The magical moment was over, and Gemma got into her car and left.

"That's another thing," Ava harrumphed. "I want to know if Bradley is dating Lahiri, and, if so, why. I'm going to have Delilah find out."

"We're going to have to buy a larger hard drive with all the mysteries to figure out between the city and this town," I said.

"Geesh!" Ava said, typing at lightning speed. "Sometimes this feels like too much."

"Then why do you keep ragging on me to get my PI license?" I whined.

"Because then it will take some weight off me." She turned her head and grinned in my direction.

"Haha, Nancy Drew. We've always done this thing together. It will just be more official."

"Yeah, but when you are official, I can dump it all on you and take the half the money." Ava held her head back and ripped out a "BWAAAHHAAHAHAAA."

I stood from sitting cross-legged on the couch and slapped her on her head.

"Ouch."

"Gemma just texted," I said, reading from my phone.

Spoke to Stella.

Ralph buying land next to the Zimmermans' farm. He was trying to work with them to buy a bit more land from them. Stella thinks the money that she found in the safe was what Ralph had borrowed for the purchase from ... whomever. She hasn't had a chance to look through all the paperwork yet.

"Well, that explains why the Zimmerman brothers weren't thrilled with Ralph," I said as I texted *Thanks* to Gemma.

"Denise should have been here fifteen minutes ago," Ava said.

"I know. I'm tired."

"Wow, you are such the night owl," Ava said, looking at the clock.

"What? I was up at four a.m., and I have to be up early tomorrow too."

"I'll call her," Ava said, tapping on her phone. She waited with it to her ear. "Not answering."

"Okay, let's go. She's hiding from us."

"I love it when you get tired and sassy," Ava said.

We drove to Denise's and rang the doorbell.

"Oh, I meant to call you and tell you I couldn't make it." Denise opened the door a few inches. She had her robe and slippers on.

"It looks like you were just ignoring us," I said, pushing my way inside. I was too tired to play games, and I felt like we had been running around in circles.

"I'm sorry," Denise said. "Hold on a minute."

Denise headed upstairs.

"She better not be climbing out a window." I crossed my arms and blew out a breath.

"You aren't playing," Ava laughed.

"Aren't you frustrated? It's like everyone is telling us half-truths, Mick is being—I don't even know what to call what he is being, we are spread so thin with the restaurant, this PI work, and I'm trying to get into these courses and get them going."

"What courses?" Denise came back down. "Sorry, I wanted to make sure the kids were occupied."

"Nothing. Denise, I have to be up early tomorrow. Now, we've known each other forever. What is going on? You looked terrified today, and it was obvious you were beating around the bush about something," I said.

"You know Darrell and I split up." Her eyebrows furrowed and she frowned. "I have custody of the kids and he's supposed to be paying child support, but he's not." Denise's face was getting red and her hands were balled into fists in frustration. "I applied for a small loan where I work, and Wanda denied me because I don't make enough to cover it." By now, Denise was shrieking. "Can you believe that?"

I shook my head. That sounded terrible, but I was still a little annoyed that she had tried to hide from us.

"You should talk to Niko about his child support," Ava said.

"I can't afford a lawyer right now," Denise moaned. "Our house payment is three months past due."

"I'm sorry to hear all of that, but what does it have to do with Betsy and a man contacting her?" I asked.

Denise stuck her tongue in her cheek then let out a huge breath. Seconds ticked by as she bit her bottom lip, then she sighed again. "Okay. You can't tell anyone this. I could get fired. The kids could be in danger."

"How are your kids in danger?" Ava asked. "Just tell us!"

"Somehow, some man, I don't know who—he calls me, knows about my financial situation. He knows my kids' names. He called and told me he had an easy way for me to make the money I need to keep my house. All I had to do was make some copies of the credit union loan coupon books and set up a few loans through him to credit union clients." Denise refused to meet our eyes.

"What? Oh my gosh!" I gasped. "Wait, but the clients don't know?"

"No, I had to mail the copies of the coupon books to a PO Box number. I'm assuming somehow he created coupon books. I set up the loans—all the official paperwork, but I don't turn it into the credit union. I mail it to the PO Box number. He's supposed to cover my back payments on the house this Friday." She started crying, then blurted out, "I messed up so bad. I'm going to get fired. I'm going to lose my kids and my house. It's all Darrell's fault!"

"Come on, just calm down. Does anyone else know about this?" I asked.

"Just you two—and whoever the guy is."

"We can figure out who he is. He had to pay for that PO Box. Can you give it to me?" Ava asked.

"Here, I wrote it down," Denise said, wiping her eyes.

"For now, don't say anything to anyone. Go about your business as normal," Ava said.

"What about when he puts the money in my account?" Denise asked.

I looked at Ava wearily. "You said this Friday?"

Denise nodded.

"That gives us a few more days. We'll get back to you," I said.

"What are you thinking?" Ava asked as we walked to the car.

"A lot of things. We need to find a bit more time this week. We're on a deadline now with that money coming to her account. We may need to get Gemma and or Bradley, Tabitha, and maybe Keith involved. I don't know—one or all of them. This is serious. Keith is a cop, but she's his sister."

Ava's cell rang.

"Who's calling at this hour?" I asked.

"Hey, babe—what?" Ava's expression changed. "Where? Are you okay?" Ava jumped in the car, pointing for me to go.

"Delilah?" I asked. Ava nodded, looking worried.

"Get to the hospital NOW!"

Chapter Eleven

"Are you okay?" Ava ran to Delilah's side.

"Yeah, it startled me more than anything. I hurt myself a little I'll be fine, though."

"Huh?"

"You both know I've been uncomfortable with Nestle having a claim to the gallery. Earlier today, I overheard him say he had a shipment coming in tonight. So, I made a point to stay at the gallery and hide to see if it came there and what it was."

"So he did this to you?" Ava looked ready to blow a fuse.

"I don't think it was him. I know his voice. It wasn't his voice. There was a shipment that came, but Nestle wasn't there. There was a knock on the back door entrance—two knocks, a pause, one knock, pause, and then three more knocks. But no one was there, so I was confused. I stayed hidden in the closet to listen to see if Nestle would show up later, but nothing. So, I went out back to find three crates marked *fragile*."

"Did you look inside?" I asked, watching as Ava paced the floor with a look like she could kill someone.

"Of course. It was olive oil. All three cases."

"So, how did you get injured?" Ava stopped pacing.

"I took a bottle out to take inside to have a closer look, and someone grabbed me from behind in a chokehold. I'm pretty sure it was a male. Deep voice. He said, 'Tell your girlfriend and her nosey friend to stay out of my business. I tried to make that clear to them before—they're not good at listening. I'd hate for you to get hurt on their behalf.'"

"Wow, he was chatty," I said, thinking it odd to say so much.

"What makes you think it wasn't Nestle? It had to be him. That had to be his shipment," Ava said in a stentorian voice.

"The height, the voice. I didn't recognize the person. Something was pressed up against my throat too, but I don't think it was a weapon. The person had gloves on, but it was weird, one of his fingers was big and bulging."

"So, he didn't hurt you?" I asked.

"No, he held me, said what he had to say, then took off. I spun around once he let me go to see if I could tell who it was. But it was dark, and all I saw was his back as he ran away. I started to chase him, but I tripped over the bottle of olive oil that I had dropped when he grabbed me. The nurse said I sprained my ankle, plus, like an idiot, I didn't use my hands to break my fall and went face-first into the concrete. I should have a nasty bruise tomorrow."

"I feel like this is all my fault," Ava said, sitting next to Delilah and stroking her long locks of hair lovingly.

"You didn't do anything. I should never have gotten involved with Nestle."

"Right, you only did that because of me." Ava had tears in her eyes—which was unusual for her.

"I'm going over there to get those crates," I said. "You stay with her."

"Oh no you don't!" Ava said. "I will not have two people I love getting hurt in one night."

"We have to find out what is so special about that oil. Remember? Tink found those caps buried in the field by M&M's, and Meiser said it was premium olive oil from Italy, specifically where his family is from."

"Call Meiser and have him go with you," Ava said.

"Yeah, right. As if." I glared at her.

"You are not going alone," Ava said.

"Who is not going alone, where?" Bradley erupted through the hospital room doorway and rushed to his sister's side.

Ava and Delilah filled him in while I looked at my watch. At this point, I realized I should give up altogether on sleep tonight.

"Okay, Bradley can you take Ava home? I'm going to go check out the crates and then head home," I said, grabbing my tote that took up the entire visitor's chair.

"Nope, I'm going with you. I agree you don't need to be in that alley alone at night. What are you? The heroine in a slasher film or something?" Bradley demanded.

Ava and Delilah laughed.

"As if you can laugh!" I pointed at Delilah as she stifled the rest of her guffaw.

I asked Bradley to drive my car so I could call Carlos, fill him in on all the events, and see if he would be willing to cover tomorrow if I could get some of my family to help with breaks. He was more than thrilled to make the extra money for his new business venture.

"Well, if you are that excited, we could use extra help through this weekend," I said. "We've got several things in the air, and many are on a deadline."

"You know me. I am not afraid of hard work, and this will help me with the loan payments."

"You will be way over forty hours. You will definitely get time and a half," I said.

"No, I'm management," Carlos said.

I laughed, "You say you need the money and argue against the extra money. We did really well at the festival, and you and your Mexican Skillet Pie were a huge reason for that. So, you are going to get time and a half. No arguments."

"Wow, can I work for you two?" Bradley asked as I hung up.

"Don't joke. Ava wrangling me into all the PI business has us not sleeping. I'm ready to hire replacements for us at the restaurant."

"It's a good thing your family is always willing to help out."

"That is one nice thing about living in a small town. Most of us who grew up here can fill in at most jobs to help out, and we trust each other."

"This is true. Although, I don't see myself ever allowing Ava to write an article and trusting her to be unbiased about anything!"

I laughed as Bradley pulled into the alley behind the gallery. "Smart!"

The headlights of my car shone on the gallery's back door. There were no crates at all. We got out of the car and looked around and in the dumpsters and walked up and down the alley.

Bradley pulled out his keys from his pocket and unlocked the gallery door.

"Huh, the alarm isn't on," Bradley said, walking into the back of the gallery.

"If she came out and got hurt, she may have forgotten to set it," I said.

"Yeah, but the door is locked. She said she drove herself to the hospital. I don't see her not setting the alarm after everything that happened."

We went looking around the entire gallery for crates—there were none.

I called Delilah, but Ava answered. "She's out. They gave her some pain meds for tonight. I brought her home with me, and she's asleep."

"Okay, well, that's good, I guess. When she wakes up, ask her if she set the alarm. It was off. Also, ask her if she kept that bottle of olive oil. There are no crates anywhere to be found."

We walked out back to my car. "I can take you home."

"What are you two doing out here?"

I shrieked and flinched, startling Bradley into a jump too.

"Good Lord, Keith, do not EVER do that again!" I yelled.

Keith was wearing the standard navy blue police uniform. "Don't do my job? I'm sorry, when

I'm driving around town and find a car in a back alleyway, I tend to want to check it out."

"Too bad you weren't here earlier when my sister was assaulted and needed you," Bradley snapped. There was not a lot of love lost between the two after the kerfuffle about which of them could be Monty's father.

"What happened?" Keith asked, taking out his cop notepad.

I filled Keith in on what happened to Betsy, what she found, that the alarm in the gallery was off. I thought very hard about telling him about Denise, but I bit my tongue for the moment. I felt *extremely* guilty, though—like I was drowning in it.

We finished up with Keith, and I drove Bradley home. Then I went home and went straight to bed.

The next morning I was awoken by Ava shaking me.

"Stooooopp," I slapped at her with spider webs in my head.

"Real nice of you to tell me that you had Carlos and some others helping out the rest of the week! I got up early, woke Delilah up, and went in to work to find out I didn't even need to be there." She had a pouted-out lip and arms crossed.

"Geesh, I'm sorry. You got home way before I did," I said, then it dawned on me that I talked to Carlos right before Ava on the phone. Whoops! Oh well, I didn't need to tell her that. It truly was an honest mistake with everything going on.

"Well, I guess I'll forgive you since you worked it out so that we have more time to figure all this out. I told Carlos and your Aunt Fern that they could call us anytime, and we could pop over and relieve them for a few hours too. Your Aunt Fern asked if she was getting overtime like Carlos."

I rolled my eyes and picked Lenny up from off my legs and handed him to Ava so I could get in the shower.

"How is Aunt Ava's Wenny Wee—how my boyee doing? Auntie Ava wuvs her Weeny wee!"

"Boy, now that you have your three, you are really turning into a cat lover," I smiled, grabbing a comfy oversized maroon sweatshirt and jeans. "I'll be out in a few."

"Okay, I'm heading home to check on Delilah, then I'll be back."

"Get some tea going, will ya?" I yelled out from the shower.

"I'm not your maid," I heard Ava mumble, and when I yelled 'WHAT?' she didn't respond.

I got out of the shower, dried my curly hair, put my make-up on in under three minutes, then threw my clothes on and ran down the steps. Ava was in the kitchen with Delilah.

"How are you doing today?" I gave her a quick hug.

"Pretty groggy. I'm not used to taking pain meds. I'm limping around."

"I told her to use the crutches they gave her," Ava said, pulling the kettle off and pouring hot water into three teacups with cinnamon-apple teabags in them. She grabbed the milk and sugar for Delilah and me.

"I know. I'm going to have to use them whether I want to or not."

We sat and drank our tea in silence, then I asked, "Hey, did Ava ask you about that bottle of olive oil?"

"Oh yeah, she told me the crates were gone and that the alarm was off. Honestly, I can't remember if I set it or not. BUT, you will be happy to know I put the bottle I fell over in my bag." She started to get up, then winced.

"I got it." Ava walked to get the crutches and put them against the table and grabbing Delilah's cloth hippie bag with fringes and tie-dyed colors.

Delilah pulled the bottle out and handed it to me. I examined the outside of the bottle and then took the lid off, looking carefully at it. "Yep, this looks to be the same kind of stuff Tink found buried in the fields by M&M's Italian Restaurant. The cap looks the same. Mick told me about it. I need to ask him to be sure."

"Hey, what's in the bottom of it?" Ava asked, squinting through the glass.

I held the bottle up to the light looking at the bottom to see something shimmering. I went to the sink and poured the oil out into a bowl through a strainer. Out popped a large diamond.

"That's not real, is it?" Ava asked, bug-eyed.

"It can't be. It's too big," I said, looking back at her in amazement.

"What is it?" Delilah asked, pushing up with her hands from the chair trying to see.

I held it out in my hand.

"Oh, my," Delilah said in a croaky voice.

Something odd welled up inside me. I wasn't sure if it was anger, confusion, annoyance, exasperation, or just being fed up. I plopped the diamond back in the oil bottle and put the lid on it. Stuffing it in my tote, I grabbed my keys, turned, and said, "I'll be back. I'm going to Mick's, and I *hope* his family is there. I'd like to know exactly what is going on here."

With that, I slammed the door behind me.

I drove on autopilot to Mick's house. When I got there, I slammed the car door and snatched the handles of my tote, marched to the door, and pounded on it. I had no idea if I had stopped for all the signs and lights or not on my way there. My mind was moving a million miles an hour.

"What on earth?" Maya said, swinging the door open.

I pushed right past her inside the foyer.

"Jolie," Mick said from the couch. He used his cane to stand up. I momentarily came out of my brain freeze to be happy to see him not using the wheelchair.

I grabbed my tote, unzipped it, and held up the olive oil bottle as I watched reactions from Maya, Maria, and Maddox.

"Is that—" Mick started limping toward me.

"Yes, the cap of this is exactly like the one I showed you that Tink found in the fields. I wanted you to look at it and tell me if it is the same, then take a look at what's in the bottom of the bottle."

"Young lady, you seem to want my son to pay attention to you. Whatever this little scheme of yours is will not work," Maddox said, standing up and walking over to swipe the bottle from Mick's hand.

"Dad, what is that in the bottom?"

"It's a diamond. Real or fake, I don't know. But it's huge. It was one bottle out of many in three crates delivered to Delilah's gallery last night where she was attacked," I said, arms crossed.

"What does that have to do with Mick or us?" Maya asked.

"Well, I never said it had anything to do with you, Maya. Mick and I have discussed this lid before, though. Also, let's just let the cat out of the bag. I know you are a mafia family."

Maria had been taking a drink of wine and coughed loudly then laughed to herself. Maddox and Maya looked like had Mick not been there, they would have considered killing me and burying the body. Me, I was done caring.

"Get out. Get OUT NOW!" Maddox insisted, grabbing me by the elbow and steering me toward the door.

"Let her go right now, Maddox," Mick used his father's first name in a stern tone. "You three get out right now. Leave us alone."

"Mick, do not be stupid. You've messed up before, and we've forgiven you. You won't be forgiven a second time," Maddox said, standing right in Mick's face, still gripping my elbow in a way that made it clear that he could break it if he really wanted to. I jerked my arm away from him and grabbed the bottle out of his hand. Maddox looked ready to slap me, but Mick took two steps forward even closer to his father's face.

"I don't need your forgiveness," Mick said in a low, dangerous voice. "I've been the fool here to think I could somehow be in this family. Now, *you* get out."

Maria set her wine glass down with a smirk, then said, "Say hi to Ava for me," and waved as she walked out.

Maya had angry tears forming in her eyes, and her typically smooth dark skin had blotched up with redness. She stared me down as she followed her husband out, slamming the door.

I took three deep breaths to get myself composed. I wasn't big on conflict and confrontation, but something had snapped. I wasn't sure what to expect from Mick or myself at this point, and while therapy had taught me to take a few steps back from this level of intense emotions, I had no plans to leave.

"Are you okay?" Mick asked, rubbing my elbow.

"Yeah. I'm trying to decide if I should apologize, and if so, for what. Not that I don't think I owe you an apology—just what all *do* I need to apologize for is more what I'm thinking ... but my mind is foggy."

"You don't owe me anything. I'm the one who should be sorry. I should have known not to get you involved with them. When Marty came after me and you could have gotten in the crosshairs of that—"

"Please don't tell me you should have left town or broken it off completely and never spoken to me again. I don't think I can take hearing that right now."

"I wish I could have done it, but I didn't. I can't. First, you were the wishy-washy one—now it's me."

"Honestly, I'm tired. I'm tired of the back and forth with us—and I mean both of us have that issue. I'm working at the restaurant, helping Ava, and now I'm signed up for PI courses to join her little part-time venture—"

"What?"

"Just don't. I can't argue right now. Look, we need to figure out if this works—and that means with my insane family, with your mafia family, with my crazy work schedule and with me getting a PI license—also, with your MS and with whatever your future decisions hold. So—" I held up my hand and shook my head to silence Mick—"let me assure you that regardless of all the back and forth over the last two years with our relationship, your MS, your family and the possible future danger that can hold for me, my hovering family, my therapy, your disapproval of my butting into dangerous things that are happening, and every other obstacle there is in our relationship—I want to be with you. No matter what. Now, you have to weigh all that and figure out what you want and be honest about what comes with it."

"Wow, I should keep going to therapy if I can sound that grown up," Mick said.

"You're going now?"

"When my family showed up, I lost it. I gave up, which is not like me. Dealing with the MS and them all at once, I became someone I didn't recognize. I felt like a little kid again."

"Yep, family will do that to you." I nodded.

He puckered his lips together while blowing out a huge breath. "What I hate more than anything is the thought of you in danger. My family can put us both in danger. You getting a PI license—danger."

"I've already been in danger. There's something bigger going on in this town. Ava and I have found ourselves in the middle of it. We are going to get to the bottom of this with or without you."

"So, you and I—we're family now," Mick said, grabbing me by the waist, dropping the cane and pulling me to him.

"That's what I want, but if you need ti—" He kissed me hard before I could finish that thought, and all of the anger I had earlier fizzled away.

I'd missed the smell of his cologne and that stupid voice he used to mimic me when I gave treats to the kitties. Truth was, when we were a couple, we were great together. He knew me well enough to know all my kooky bits and how I love to give inanimate objects voices and personify them. Mick knew the smartest thing to do was to play along.

What I missed the most was when he nuzzled the back of my neck like he was doing right now, sending internal shivers up and down my body.

A little later, I was taking Meiser back to meet up with Ava and Delilah (after a lengthy make-out session to make up for lost time.) "So, you know me—I need to know all the deets."

Mick laughed. "So, yeah, I'm seeing Tabitha, taking the meds and waiting for them to get in my system to help with the mood issues—she has given me some things to try between now and when the meds kick in—but I feel like you can help a lot with that."

I wriggled my eyebrows. "Oh yeah, I can definitely do my part to keep you happy!"

"I do the first infusion tomorrow. I'd love for you to go with me."

"I'm there. You and I need to catch up on—talking," I said, giggling as my mind wandered to other things.

"I brought a change of clothes and left extra food for the turds before we left my place," Mick said, referring to Stewart and Lucky.

"There's a lot I need to tell you. My uncles, the murder, what is happening in this town, and so much more."

"Speaking of the case, I've made up my mind to call Teddy and see if I can do some desk work until I see if this new medicine works."

"So, we can be partners," I said in glee.

"Partners in everything." He laid his hand on my leg, and there was that feeling again.

I stopped at Cast Iron Creations to check in on Carlos before heading home. He was busy prepping for dinner. Magda was up front. "Hey Magda, you haven't been here all day, have you?"

"Nope, just came in five minutes ago. Your Aunt Fern was here. She headed over to eat with the mayor and said she'd be back. I told her to take her time because I had a five-hour shift, but she said something about you paying her overtime?" Magda looked at me suspiciously.

"She isn't getting overtime. Carlos is because he is helping out and putting in a lot of hours this week to do Ava and me a solid," I said.

"You know I can always use more money," Magda said.

"I never know what your college schedule is. Ava has me doing some PI work with her, and we have some things we have to take care of in the next few days."

"I'll talk to your Aunt Fern and see if she can work around my classes and I'll be here the rest of the time. Carlos and I make a good team, kind of like you and Ava," Magda smiled.

Ugh, my stomach dropped. I didn't know if Magda knew Carlos was leaving or not and if that meant she'd follow him to his restaurant. I didn't think it was my place to share his plans, so I didn't say anything.

"I'm going to run back to the kitchen to check on Carlos. Get yourself anything to drink. Do you want some food?" I asked Mick.

"Um, yeah, I'll take a to-go box of anything that is back there. I'm not picky."

"Kind of like with your women?"

"Yeah, I'll take any old woman," Mick laughed.

"Awww, I'm so happy you two figured it out. You belong together, and it's kind of dumb neither of you knew that," Magda said, holding a coffee pot in one hand and wiping down the counter with the other. She walked away to greet a customer.

"Wow, out of the mouths of babes," I laughed.

"Leave it to a nineteen-year-old to put us in our place," Mick said.

"Hey Carlos, how's it going? You dying for a break yet?"

"Nope, I'm using this to help prepare me for long days and nights when I start my business. I've got everything prepped and a few dishes in the oven for customers. Do you care if I run out for about ten minutes?"

"Take an hour or two. I can cover for you like you are for me."

"Nah, I just need to run a quick errand, and I'm going to grab a soda. I ate a little bit ago. There's a bunch of Carlos' Heavens to Murgatroyd Cast Iron Queso dip in the fridge."

"Great, I'm going to get some to go."

I washed my hands, checked out the food in the oven, looked over the prep for the night, and got some food ready for Mick, Delilah, Ava, and me for later. Next, I started prepping for tomorrow morning. I figured it was the least I could do, so maybe Carlos could not have to come in as early.

I grabbed some eggs, bacon, and sourdough to put aside on the breakfast shelf in the refrigerator. Next, I made up the fried donut batter and separated them into several dozen small balls, put them on trays to rise, and was covering them when Carlos came back.

"Oh wow, thank you!" Carlos exclaimed.

"Hey, you can sleep in a little tomorrow. Also, feel free to close a bit earlier tonight and open later tomorrow since you are taking on so much. All I ask is that you put a note on the front door, so the customers know."

"Your family has been helping. Your aunt and grandma have come in to give me breaks and gave me their numbers to call them. Mary came in when I had to run out earlier for a half hour. Don't worry, I'm fine."

"See, all these people will pitch in to help you too with your restaurant—including me and Ava."

I grabbed our food and headed up front where I saw Mick talking to Zander Zimmerman. Zander seemed to be upset and flustered, but the conversation was ending when I walked up.

"Hi, Jolie," Zander said dully.

"Everything okay?" I asked.

"Yeah, see ya," and he headed out.

"What was that all about?" I asked.

"I was asking him about the argument he and his brother had with Ralph by the B&B. He told me Ralph wanted to buy some of their farmland. They refused and were working to buy out the plot of land he was going to purchase. So, Zander questioned if Ralph was trying to poison one of them and accidentally got the desserts mixed up and ate it himself."

Chapter Twelve

Mick and I walked into my house, and I called Ava. She was at her place with Delilah, and she said Peggy, Gemma, and Bradley were there, too.

"Not Lahari, right?" I asked.

"Nope, not here," Ava said in a clipped tone. I assumed Bradley was standing nearby.

"Okay, we will be over in a minute. I grabbed a bunch of food from our restaurant. Do you have tortilla chips there?"

"Yes, who is 'we'?"

"Oh," I looked over. Mick was sitting at the table, petting Lenny, and Bobbi Jo was on the table. He was rubbing her neck while she head-butted him. "Mick's with me."

"Yeah, aaannddd ...?"

"Lots to discuss—" I started, but Mick had reached for the phone.

"Hey, Ava. Basically, Jolie came to my house and blatantly accused my family of being in the mob and trying to smuggle diamonds in olive oil. My dad physically tried to remove her, which set me off. There was a huge confrontation. Long story short, I kicked them out. She and I made up in a really fun way—not that I'd kiss and tell, but we both know she will tell you. And—we are officially on again." He was grinning at me as I tried grabbing the phone from him throughout that entire spiel.

Mick held up an arm to keep me from grabbing the phone as he listened, then laughed out loud and hung up.

"What did she say?"

"It's between Ava and me. If you and I are a couple, then she and I need to have our own relationship too." He gave me an alluring smile.

I rolled my eyes, grabbed the food and some extra tortilla chips and tortillas in case we needed more. I had also bought some pouches of various margarita mixes that I keep in the freezer. I put them in a bag to take over.

When we got to Ava's, she and I got all the food and drinks ready in her kitchen. "Sounds like you caused quite a scene with Meiser's family. Not even I would have called them out on being mafia to their faces."

"What can I say? I snapped."

"Seems like it worked in your favor," Ava said, nodding at Mick, who was sitting next to Peggy, offering condolences for her loss.

"It wasn't like that was my plan," I said, adding some salt to the rims of the glasses and filling them with slushy strawberry yumminess.

"Everyone knew you both would be back together sooner or later."

"Yeah, yeah. I'm hoping we've hit a place where we both are going to stop being so stubborn and stop trying to protect each other from ourselves and just be together."

"Why don't you both give that a try?" Ava grinned.

"Thanks!"

We carried the reheated food and drinks out to the group, and Ava wrangled up the kittens and put them in what she called their 'playpen,' which consisted of a baby gate that divided the family room from the kitchen and another at the dining room. Ava sat by one gate so she could play when they came near. They had the run of the house other than the room we were currently in so that we could eat in peace.

"So, how are you dealing with things, Peggy?" Bradley asked.

"Bradley," Delilah said as if he was being insensitive.

"It's fine, Delilah. It's a lot, to be honest. I'm still confused by it all. I've known Ralph for several years, only from eating his pizza. We only started dating a few months ago and getting to know each other better. It's strange to me that Stella started working for him just a few months ago and he left everything to her. Not that I expected anything. But then there's everything with Tonya."

"Did you tell them the news?" Gemma asked Peggy.

Peggy shook her head.

"What's up?" Ava asked, grabbing her laptop and opening it up to take some notes.

"Tonya's husband, Noah, owns an investment firm in the city. He makes a lot of money. Gemma did a little digging and found out that Noah is using his firm's money to help Cardinal with his plans for gentrifying parts of the city."

"I think I understand gentrification better than I do urban sprawl—the first seems to be something done by politicians to improve an area of the city." I used finger quotes around the word "improve." "But urban sprawl seems like it is supposed to be something that just naturally occurs. What's happening in Leavensport doesn't feel natural at all."

"Um, gentrification is how the place changes," Gemma said. "Displacement is when politicians or whoever it is, come in and begin moving people to get them out of an area. The mayor is playing it smart, being the face of creating jobs, providing better housing, and other things for middle and upper-class citizens. He's using others to displace the homeless and those that are working-class behind the scenes."

"She's right," Bradley added, "and what's happening here in Leavensport is known as 'leapfrog development,' which is a type of urban sprawl. Some say it means taking a lot of vacant land and finding shortcuts to infrastructure to create fast-growing economies. Mayor Nalini is presenting it this way for positive optics."

"How do you both know so much about all of this?" Ava asked.

"Jolie, remember you saying how we all pitch in to help in our small town? Well, since Gemma and I both love technology, we've been doing a lot of chatting online since we met, and both of us are big research buffs interested in what's happening in our place of residence. So, we are working on some articles together."

Delilah smiled at Ava and me.

"But—" I started until Ava gave me a look that clearly said *shut up*. She must have known I was getting ready to ask about Lahiri.

"But what?" Gemma asked.

I allowed my misstep to take me to other thoughts that had been floating around. "So, Ralph had twenty-five thousand and was trying to purchase land and add a bit more by purchasing some of the Zimmerman's farmland—they, in turn, were trying to keep their land and purchase the plot he wanted as well. The question that keeps floating in my mind is, did Ralph's death have to do with the purchase of the land? If so, is that tied to the Zimmermans, or to the bigger picture of this entire leapfrog development tied in to Tri-City?"

Ava was typing away. "Also, we need to know more about Tonya. Jolie felt she was messing around with Cardinal. Then Stella saw her in the car with Ralph. Stella is left his business. Is there something in all that connected to it?"

"Let me go talk to Teddy and see what I can find out, since I'm not officially working for the department right now but trying to get my job back." Mick used his cane to walk toward me and leaned down to kiss me and headed outside with his phone.

"Well, he is just smitten, isn't he?" Bradley teased. "I've never known that man to be willing to bend the law."

"He's not officially working for the law right now," I said.

"Hey gals, it's getting late. We best be heading back to the city," Peggy said, yawning.

"Thanks for the information. If you find anything else out, let us know. I think we are headed in the right direction. We just need to do a bit more digging." Ava stood to hug Peggy.

"Yeah, I'm going to get Delilah home too. She's looking sleepy," Bradley said.

After everyone was out of Ava's house, we put the food away and cleaned up and let the fur babies have the run of the whole place again. I texted Mick when I didn't see him outside. He texted back that he went to my house to have a conversation with Teddy on the phone.

"Okay, Delilah said something at the hospital that has bothered me. The person that attacked her said they tried to warn us *before*." I looked at Ava questioningly.

"Yeah, I assumed that was whoever took the money from you."

"I thought that too. But the money seems to be tied into what happened to Ralph. I feel like what happened to Ralph is its own crime, but it's also tied into something larger. I don't know if that makes any sense."

"I hear you. I never thought of that—so you think whoever attacked Delilah because of the olive oil was different than the person who took the gym bag of money from you."

"I do."

"Oh crap, I never uploaded the pictures I took of the money," Ava said, looking for her phone as Mick came back inside.

"What did you find out?" Ava asked, grabbing her phone, a cable to connect to the laptop, and starting the uploads.

"Well, first off, Teddy and I agree that I should wait two or three weeks after I start the Tysabri to see if anything changes and that will give all the different meds I'm on time to kick in. Then we'll reconvene. In the meantime, I can consult as needed."

"That sounds promising," I said. "Besides, when is the last time you took a vacation?"

"I take a day or two off here and there. Like you can talk."

"Anyway, did you find anything useful out?" Ava barked.

Mick and I chuckled. "He's been looking into everything. He found out that Tonya's husband knew about her affairs with Cardinal and Ralph. He's already brought him in for questioning, but he seems to have an alibi, so Teddy didn't have anything to hold him on. He wasn't at the festival. I guess Betsy is safe for now. You gave her good advice, telling her to hire Niko. He is building a case that she had no motive to poison Ralph in case Teddy decides to call her back in for more questioning. She only had opportunity, but there are many other people who had opportunity as well."

"Good, I know Teddy didn't want to believe she had anything to do with it," I said.

"Since the three of us are all here– Ava, open the folder about the land for sale."

"Got it," she said.

"Do you think your family is involved in having that olive oil shipped here to smuggle in diamonds?" I asked Meiser.

Ava looked worried. "Nothing like testing the relationship immediately."

Mick laughed, "Yes, I do. Did you see their reaction?"

"But Delilah said she overheard Nestle saying an order was being delivered to the gallery. So, is your family somehow tied to Nestle? You said something about it before."

"You wouldn't have any wine, would you?" Mick asked.

Ava got up and went to get some, "Red or white?"

"Red, please."

She brought a glass out to him. "You'll have to hold onto the glass. If you sit anything with a long stem down anywhere, the kittens will knock it over."

"So, my family belongs to the Sicilian mob. Nestle belongs, or at least he used to belong, to the Canadian mob. He and my father have done business in the past, and that has led to him working with my brothers as well."

"Do you know he's related to Lydia?" I asked.

"Yes, she told me."

"She said she didn't know until recently that he is her uncle. Is that why her father is in jail?" I asked.

"I don't know the entire story with her dad. She found out he changed his last name kind of for the same reasons I did—so that makes me think he wanted nothing to do with it."

"She always thought he was in jail because of drugs," Ava said.

"So, if your family is having diamonds smuggled here for some reason and working with Nestle, then that makes me wonder if any of them are connected with the Perezes or the Valendros from Santo Domingo."

"I had the same thought while we were there. It's like a spider web of mafia activity, all leading to Leavensport. There are too many things happening for it to be a coincidence."

"Agreed, that's why Tabitha, Teddy, and I have been working on it for a while now," Meiser said.

Ava and I looked hard at each other.

"How long?" I asked.

"That's the entire reason why I came here to begin with."

Chapter Thirteen

"I thought I was the reason you came here," I said to Mick once we were back at my place. I was pulling the comforter down and tossing the extra pillows to the floor from the bed.

"Someone thinks highly of herself," Mick said, grabbing pillows from his side.

"You know what I mean. You were working in the city and moved here when we started our flirting."

"I moved to work in the city because my brother was the mayor. Then, I found out he and Nestle were looking into land here in Leavensport. I talked to Teddy about it, and that's when Ellie was murdered."

"Well, I did not know that because you never explained it." I picked up a pillow and threw it at him.

"I think we will find out the longer we stay together, the more things we'll realize we need to tell each other."

"So, Tabitha is a therapist, right?"

"Yes, but like me, she came here for other reasons. She does need to make money, and that is why she started the practice, but she's also doing some other things for the FBI too."

"So, she's undercover as a therapist? Have I been telling my darkest secrets to a fake therapist?" My mouth dropped open.

"NO! She is what she says she is, and she also is more," Mick said, throwing the pillow back across the bed at me.

"This is all so confusing!" I had brought my laptop upstairs, grabbed it, and sat cross-legged in bed, opening it up.

"What are you looking at?"

"Pulling up our I Spy Slides," I said.

"Huh?"

"That's what Ava and I call them. When everything happened with Ellie, we needed a way to track everything, because we didn't know what we were doing. Of course, Ava needed an official name—I'm sure that contributed to why she eventually became a PI. So, we share the PowerPoint."

I pulled it up and opened the different folders from each case we worked. Mick grabbed the laptop and began looking through all the slides and the notes of the past crimes we had worked and solved. He giggled a few times.

"What's so funny?"

"Some of these pictures you both took. You are terrible at being subtle. Then some of the notes are hilarious!"

"Yeah, well, it worked, did it not?" I squared my shoulders and raised my chin.

"Hey, I'm not taking anything away from either of you. In all honesty, this is incredible for two people who have zero training in any of this stuff. Also, as I look from one to the next, I can see a ton of growth in how you both think and process things."

I got excited by his compliments. "Yeah, and honestly, Ava is getting pretty amazing after she took those PI courses and got her license. I've learned so much from her the last few months, and it's got me excited to learn more." At this point, I went from crossed legs to sitting on my knees, leaning over him to look at the slides.

Mick reached out and kissed me on the cheek, then said, "You're cute."

"It's a blessing and a curse," I said, reaching for another kiss.

"And so humble."

I grinned as humbly as possible as he went in for more kissing, but I happened to glance at the computer screen at a picture of the current case that was up, and my head whipped around.

"What?" Mick asked. I pointed at the screen. It was a picture we had taken at the festival, and Tonya Morrison was visible in the background.

"Who is that man Tonya is snuggled up to by that tree? How many men is she sleeping with?"

"That's her husband, Noah—hey, wait!"

Mick and I looked wide-eyed at each other.

"He supposedly had an air-tight alibi and wasn't at the festival. Also, they are pretty close to Ralph's booth. If he knew his wife was sleeping with Ralph—" I mused.

"Yeah, looks like you and Ava have found crucial evidence yet again. This will make him suspect number one."

"Who are you calling?" I asked.

"Teddy, so he can go pick him up for questioning."

The next morning, Mick and I were getting ready for his first infusion treatment. I was nervous for him, but he didn't seem to be.

"So, for the sake of honesty—"

"Oh no, should you really tell me something right before all this?"

"It's not about us."

"Who is it about?"

"Keith's sister, Denise. She messed up—it's pretty big," I said, getting the water boiling in the kettle.

"What did she do?"

I proceeded to get our tea and sat down, explaining the loans to Mick. His face fell as he listened. He shook his head and clenched his jaw.

"We have to tell Teddy and Keith about this, Jolie. This isn't something to mess with. We have to find out who this man is—"

"But Denise is a single mom with kids. I know she screwed up, but her kids. She was worried about their safety. I don't want to see her in jail."

Mick kept his head still and blinked as he thought. "One thing at a time. You said this happens in a couple of days. Let me get this treatment and think about it more. We will tell them, but I need to think about all the angles here."

"Okay, let's go."

"So, this will take a couple of hours. Supposedly, I can drive myself afterwards if you have other things to do."

"Nope, I've got the laptop, and Ava is going to stop by if that's okay."

"The more, the merrier." Mick rolled his eyes.

"It's not a secret, is it?" I never thought to ask that question.

"No, everyone has seen me in a wheelchair, and everyone knows everything here anyway."

"Well, except who killed Ralph."

We were at the clinic, and Mick was all hooked up for his treatment. Ava had just come in with Keith. I texted and asked her to bring him. I told Mick I was doing that so we could discuss the Denise thing with him. He and Keith seemed to be able to keep a professional relationship, but I still sensed tension between the two. Mick didn't seem thrilled to have Keith see him in a vulnerable state.

"Hey, man." Keith was wearing faded light blue jeans, an Ohio State Buckeye sweatshirt, and rubbing one hand through his wavy blonde hair as he walked over to Mick, shaking the hand that wasn't hooked up the I.V. "So, Teddy tried to bring Noah in for questioning, but no one can find him."

"What? Did he know we were onto him?" Mick asked.

"Teddy wasn't sure. He called the department in Tri-City, and they sent a deputy to his home with a warrant. He wasn't there. Tonya was, and I guess she was ticked. They've got a BOLO out on him."

"Hey, I'm afraid we have some bad news for you," Mick changed the subject. "Take a seat."

I was the one who broke the news to Keith. He looked mortified and put his face in his hands, leaning over his knees and rubbing his hands over his face in anguish.

"What in the hell was she thinking? I could have helped her with money!"

"She probably didn't want to ask her little brother," I said.

"Plus, I know what you make. You couldn't afford to help her and her kids and take care of yourself," Mick said.

"I would have figured it out," Keith said.

"That's probably her line of thinking," Ava said.

Just then, Baggy, the troubadour, came into the room of people getting treatments, sporting a vintage maroon houndstooth blazer, gray t-shirt, holey jeans, old cowboy boots, his Fedora, saxophone, and a scroll that he dramatically whipped out with one hand as the paper unrolled.

Baggy cleared his throat, took a bow, and began:

Seasons of the living to be read.

Living day to day giving more than we take.

Roller coaster riding the wave.

Seasons change per the day.

May your health lead you astray.

He then grabbed his sax and began a jazzy tune.

Keith, Ava, Mick, and I all looked at each other completely confused.

"Was that supposed to rhyme?" I asked anyone within earshot. I noticed other people in the clinic looked equally baffled.

"Forget rhyming—there was supposed to at the very least have some sort of meaning, right?" Keith asked.

"At least he's good at playing the sax," Ava said, grabbing a dollar out of her purse and taking it to put in the cap Baggy had laid by his feet. He nodded in response, finished his tune, and bowed as other people left change, smiled awkwardly at him, and left.

"Well, this town gets stranger and stranger," Mick said.

"So, I have to tell Teddy. She could go to jail," Keith moaned.

"I say we all talk to Teddy. See if we can come up with a deal where Denise helps us figure out who this guy is for lesser or no time."

"She'll be fired for sure," Keith said.

"We'll all help out. She can work for us part-time," I said, as Keith smiled appreciatively at me.

"If Teddy lets me come back full-time, I'll need another assistant manager at the restaurant. Mrs. Seevers has told me she has to cut back to part-time," Mick said.

"Why?" I asked.

"Unlike you, I don't always pry into peoples' private lives," Mick said.

"Yes, you do. You're a detective," Ava said. "Don't think because you are getting this infusion that anyone in this room is going to cut you a break!"

I stifled a laugh, but Keith let his laughout, then said, "Yeah, man. Small towns are the worst at times, but then you have people like these two who will keep you honest."

"I guess I was acting the victim for a while there," Mick laughed.

"You think?" Ava hooted, cracking up.

I started giggling, then Meiser said, "What are you laughing at? You're just jealous that since we are a hot item again that now Ava and I have developed a friendship as warped as what you two have."

"It's totally true. I'm completely jelly!"

"That's it!" Dr. Delagada popped in as the nurse began unhooking Mick.

"Really? I don't feel any different," Mick said, standing slowly to stretch his legs.

"You won't, for a bit. You don't need to bring a bunch of people. You can see you don't feel much different. You can drive yourself," she said, making a few notes on Mick's chart.

"This is my fault. I wanted to be here for the first session and invited a couple of people for some work purposes," I said.

"Okay, well, any questions before I head out?" she asked.

"I don't think so," Mick said.

"He comes back when?" I asked.

"He should get the infusion every twenty-eight days to start out. Different people notice things at different stages—if he finds he is feeling better sooner than later, then that's a good sign," she said.

"Okay, so that works out to twelve infusions a year?" I asked, knowing how horrible I was with math.

"If he gets one every twenty-eight days, it will be thirteen a year. If it's working well after the first two sessions, then we may wait six to eight weeks between infusions."

"Okay, thanks," I said as she power-walked away.

I dropped Mick off at his place so he could take care of his fur monsters then called Stella on my way home.

"So, you had us all worried," I said when she answered.

"I know. I need to stop doing that, especially with everything that's been going on," Stella said. "I'm sorry I had you all worried. That wasn't my intention. When I was in high school, a bunch of us used to go hiking regularly. We found this old abandoned tiny camper up a cliff—it was always a big mystery how anyone got it up there. Anyway, you can imagine a group of teens finding a little hideaway. I've always used it as a place to hide when life gets to be too much."

"Hey, you don't have to explain it to me. I used to take days off to hide-out from everyone when I got overwhelmed."

"Yeah, but you didn't run out of town without telling a soul, did you?"

"No, I didn't go that far. But between Ava and my family, they would have demanded the police department, FBI, CIA, and every other acronymed, police-related force go out to find me."

"It must be nice having so many people love you so much." Stella sounded disheartened.

Yet again, I stuck my stupid foot in my mouth. "You had people going to the police about you, lady. You *are* loved by people in the city and here in town. We were all texting, calling, leaving messages for you, then, once we didn't know what else to do, contacting the police."

"I guess." She perked up.

"Like it or not, you are loved. Get used to it."

"I don't feel like I deserve it right now. Peggy is the one who introduced me to Ralph. I worked for her first. Then, I catch him with that nasty woman, and I don't tell Peggy. I love her so much. She's been nothing but kind to me, and this is how I repay her. Now, she was dating him, knew him longer, and he leaves *me* everything?"

"Peggy adores you, and she doesn't blame you at all. Believe me. We've talked. You are good with her. We are all happy for you, Stella. Not happy about what happened to Ralph, mind you, but happy for you."

"I never in my life thought I'd own a business. I had no idea what I wanted to do with my life. I was just figuring out how to be *me*—so, figuring out a career wasn't something I was contemplating at the moment. This would help me out a lot with money, though. I feel like a jerk for saying that."

"I get it. And you know a lot of people who own businesses. We can all help you with decision-making while you are learning the ropes," I said. "Hey, when you caught Tonya with Ralph in his car—er—this is a weird question."

"Go ahead, I know you and Ava are investigating, and Peggy is paying you. I'll do whatever I can to help her and figure out who did this to Ralph."

"Was Tonya on top of him, or was he on top of her? I have a feeling Tonya is the type to be with different guys even though she's married. I didn't know Ralph that well, and it seems like Peggy is confused by it all too."

Stella was silent on the other end of the phone. I assumed she was taking her time to relive the moment. "He was in the driver's seat, and she was leaning over him from the passenger seat. I know that because it did match what he told me later. It's part of the reason I wanted to believe him."

"Okay, that helps," I said, making a mental note.

"There was something else that was strange."

"What's that?"

"It was night, but across the street, I saw someone in a hoodie watching them with binoculars."

"You wouldn't happen to know if it was a man or woman, would you?"

"No, like I said, it was late. Honestly, I didn't think a lot about it until now, as strange as that sounds. It was a beautiful night—clear skies with lots of stars, and they seemed to be looking at the sky at first. Then I noticed the binoculars moved to the car. I guess I just thought someone stumbled across a chance to be a Peeping Tom."

"Thanks, Stella, I just pulled into my drive. I'll talk to you later."

Very interesting. I made a beeline for Ava's place and checked the door—unlocked.

"Hey, you are the one always telling me to keep my doors locked!"

"Yeah, well, no one has tried to kill me yet."

"*Yet* being the key word!"

I grabbed a Coke Zero from her fridge, popped the can, and took a few swigs. "So, I just spoke to Stella on the phone. Load up the I Spy Slides."

As Ava got her laptop, she said, "Why did you tell Meiser about our secret slides?"

I felt a twinge of guilt. "We were talking about the case last night. Oh, and I realized we have a picture of Noah, Tonya's husband with her at the festival, which breaks his alibi!"

I hoped that bit of information would help her forgive me.

"I already know that," she said.

"How? Also, how do you know I told Mick about the slides?" I asked hands on hips.

"Oh, well, after you dropped him off, I went to his place and got some lunch."

My mouth fell open, and I almost dropped my can of Coke. "Why?" I asked, annoyed.

"I wanted to ask him some questions without you around." She bit her lower lip, opening the folder.

"What kind of questions?"

"None of your beeswax! You don't need to know everything."

"If it concerns my best friend, my boyfriend, and myself—then yeah, I think I do need to know," I put the can down and reached down for Lily and picked her up. "Plus—" I started, but Lily reached up and put her front paw over my mouth, shushing me.

Ava cracked up laughing when she didn't remove the paw from my mouth.

I put her down, "Did you train her to do that?"

"You should know better than anyone you can't train a cat. That's why they are superior to dogs—they are independent with their own personalities."

"Hey, I love dogs too!" I protested.

"Me too, but cats are better!"

"Again, what questions?"

"He may or may not be my source for some information," Ava mumbled under her breath.

"WHAT? I practically have to force him to tell me anything, and he is providing you with information on cases? Just this case or past cases?"

"Since I got my PI license, he's been helping me get some information. He helped me out a bit last May and with this case too."

I shook my head and used my hand to attempt to whack some sense into my brains. "I cannot believe this. So, you two were sharing case information all this time—and when he and I weren't together?"

Ava shrugged. "As a PI, I can get away with some things that he legally can't do. No one else should ever know this."

"Oh my gosh. I've been floored before—but this!"

"Hey, don't even start on the guilt train with me, Jolie Lynn Tucker! You and Delilah hid stuff from me for a long time before you 'fessed up." Ava's long, multi-colored beaded necklaces that she wore to accent her oversized neon-yellow sweatshirt and tights swung as she spun her desk chair. Ugh, I hated it when she made a good point. I ignored this information for now and summarized the conversation I just had with Stella.

"Do you think the person with binoculars was Tonya's husband?" Ava went right along with ignoring the elephant in the room.

"It makes sense to me. Like I said before, I think whatever happened to Ralph was more personal."

"But we can't rule out that it is tied in with the mafia, either," Ava said.

"That's true. You know, Meiser complimented us when he looked over the slides last night. He said we had grown a lot in our detecting methods since investigating Ellie's murder."

"Yeah, we talked about that too."

"So, are you two dating now?"

"Don't be dumb. You know I don't swing that way! Plus, you and Delilah were being all weirdly close before!"

"Oy, so, if I try to bring up this you-and-Mick thing, you are immediately going to rub me and Delilah in my face?"

"Yes," she said in a DUH tone.

"So make a note of this, is the person who poisoned Ralph the same person who took the money from me? Also, is that the same person who attacked Delilah? I say no—maybe who took the money from me and who killed Ralph are the same, but not the one who attacked Delilah."

Ava nodded, typing it in. "FYI, Keith was heading to Denise's to confront her. She's probably going to hate us."

"Great, I can add one more person to the list who wants to murder me."

Chapter Fourteen

The next day we went back to work at Cast Iron Creations to give Carlos and Magda a much-needed rest. It was slower than usual, and, being paranoid as I am, I couldn't help wonder if people saw Ava and I were back, and they were staying away until Carlos came back with his tasty Mexican recipes.

Lydia came in with Monty in a stroller. I had to admit he was adorable. Ava and I found ourselves doing something we swore we'd never do, which was leaning over him and cooing and awing.

"Do either of you want to hold him?" Lydia picked him up and held him out to us.

We both panicked. Baby talk was one thing.

"Um, I don't really know how to hold a baby," I said, feeling foolish.

"How have you never held a baby?" Lydia asked.

"I'm an only child who never babysat."

"I have a sister, but she's close to my age. Not a baby person, sorry!" Ava was more blunt than I was.

"Okay, but you both will hold him before all is said and done," Lydia threatened.

I smiled uncomfortably and headed behind the counter to look over all the notes Carlos, Magda, Grandma Opal, Mom, and Aunt Fern had left.

Grandma left a four-page letter that began with a scathing critique of how I cared for my skillets and the proper way to do it. That led into three pages about Shelly and how she's always been a troublemaker even back when she started dating Uncle Eddie. She gave me no specifics, which seemed odd for three pages worth of babbling—but that's my grandma for you.

I looked up when I heard Lydia raise her voice. A half-second later, I heard Monty's shrill cry, probably triggered by his mom's distress. Jackson Nestle stood by Lydia, asking to hold little Monty.

Lydia immediately joined the protective mom's club and shielded Monty from him, holding a hand over Monty's head and turning her body away from Nestle.

"Hey, she obviously doesn't want you around the baby. You need to leave," I said, walking between him and Lydia.

"What if I want to order some food?" Nestle eyed me angrily.

"Ava, we just ran out of all of our food, didn't we?" I yelled back at her.

"Yeah, there are other restaurants in town, though. Good thing you are helping Mayor Cardinal and the ex-mayor of Tri-City to buy up some land here for more restaurants. You'll have to buy up all the land in the world to find someone to serve you!"

"I feel you two have been warned on many occasions to mind your own business," Nestle said. I froze. *He wasn't even pretending that he wasn't involved in the attack in the alley by the gallery!*

"What did you just say?" Ava came bolting up in his face. "If you dare to touch my girlfriend ever again, you will regret the day you were born."

"Is that a threat?" Nestle grinned, unaffected.

"I don't threaten people. You know, you aren't the only one to rub elbows with the mafia," Ava said.

I couldn't believe she said that! I quickly changed the subject. "What are your thoughts on premium olive oil? Have you heard the term *agromafia* before?"

Nestle's lip curled, and he grunted a comment I wouldn't repeat and stormed out.

"Thank you both," Lydia said, bouncing Monty on her shoulder to quiet him.

Ava stomped back to the kitchen. I knew she preferred to be alone when she was trying to cool off.

I took a deep breath. "Hey, Lydia?" She looked at me, eyebrows raised, still bouncing the baby. "Why is the father of the baby a secret? Mick and I are back together. I can tell he knows, but he won't tell me because he wants to respect your priv—"

Suddenly, Tonya Morrison came barreling into the restaurant. She stomped up to me and got right in my face, pointing a finger that touched my nose. "My life is NONE of your business!" she yelled. "John has been nothing but good to Elijah, and with all of your nosing around, he's thinking about firing *both* of us!"The baby started to wail again, and Lydia quickly put him back in the stroller and hustled out, waving at me.

"First off, remove that finger from my face," I said, glancing around and happy for the first time today that the restaurant was empty.

Tonya took two steps back, glaring at me. "You don't know anything about my life. Noah was unfaithful to me *way* before I ever was to him. Our relationship has been over for years—it's platonic at this point. It works for us, and that is none of your business. I've worked for John in one capacity or another for nineteen years now, and I'm the one who helped get him into the position of mayor. That helped Noah with his business and vice versa."

"Does Noah know your relationship is over?" Ava said, coming from the back.

"Again, none of your business either!"

"It is our business if your husband is going to go around poisoning everyone you decide to make out with!"

"What on earth are you talking about?"

"Noah said he had an alibi. Did you lie to help him cover the fact that he was at the festival the day Ralph was poisoned?" I asked.

"How do you know he was there?"

"We're PI's." Ava crossed her arms.

A table of five came into the restaurant at that moment, and Ava and I took several steps back and smiled at the customers. Ava walked over to get them seated and set up.

Tonya took a step closer to me and said, "Stay out of my business, you little witch," and she stormed out.

After work, Ava came to my place so we could talk about the progress of the case. I ran upstairs for the package I ordered last week and came back with an enormous whiteboard.

"What is that?" Ava asked.

"Listen, I think every single crime that's happened in Leavensport in the past few years is part of something bigger. Since you and Mick are so close now, you know he came here to investigate his brother when he was mayor of Tri-City. You probably already know that Tabitha is here undercover for the FBI, too."

Ava's eyes bugged out. "What?"

I had to admit I got some satisfaction for knowing something she didn't. I told her what Mick shared and grabbed a dry-erase marker. I began listing the crimes, starting with Ellie Siler.

"But we know who killed her—that had nothing to do with a bigger plot," Ava said, referring to when we found sweet old Ellie dead outside our restaurant in the alley.

"Just go with me for now." Next, I listed Lou, who was found dead in his home.

"After Lou is Pria," Ava said woefully. Pria was a teen advocate in Tri-City. She's how we met Stella. We both liked Pria a lot.

"Then the mess with your family in Santo Domingo leading to Darla and Mod last May," I wrote as I said it.

I wrote out the words 'gentrification' and 'urban sprawl/leapfrog development' at the top of the board, with the list going horizontal at the bottom of the whiteboard.

Ava grabbed a red dry-erase marker and went from Pria to gentrification as I nodded in agreement. I grabbed the marker from her and went from Lou's name to 'leapfrog development.' Ava grabbed a green marker to draw a line from her family to 'urban sprawl.' She wrote in between the list of victims and the categories we created

'Canadian Mafia,' 'Sicilian Mafia,' and 'Dominican Republic Mafia."

I stood back and stared at the board, then thought about all the lines we had just drawn. "Okay, I'm adding the word 'Mafia' alone for those we don't know if there is a connection there," I added the word to the right side and made a line from Ellie's name there.

"I think we can move every victim's name to the 'general' mafia category except my dad. We can make a line to the DR Mafia with him. It's unfortunate that my dad ever met Ron Renee and got mixed up with all that."

"Yeah, but your family has no mafia ties," I said.

"Write Denise down as a victim and Ralph," Ava said.

"Duh, yeah, right. There's so much here."

I took a breath and thought about each incident.

"Several of these peoples' deaths can be tied to the sale of the land here in Leavensport. Ellie was a business owner, causing Betsy to take over and needing a loan. Lou was onto something with the land for sale when he was murdered. Pria was fighting the displacement of the homeless and advocating for the teen center to stay where it was. Your dad was blackmailed. Darla and Mod's deaths are difficult. They were from the city, and Lahiri is Mayor Nalini's niece, but we don't have anything to show he's in on anything other than growing the economy here," I said.

"Yeah, but the connection is Lahiri, who was involved with those girls. Alyssa is gone, and there is more to it all there, too."

We began drawing lines and writing in different theories. By the time we came up with about six different theories and noted them all on the slides and the whiteboard, we were both beat.

"Ow, my brains!" I said, rubbing my forehead.

"Who knows how long all of this has been going on? We need to prioritize. For Peggy, we need to find out who killed Ralph and why. That's number one on the list."

"Yeah, then it will be the holidays—that will be a whole other thing to survive," I said, knowing Halloween, Thanksgiving, and Christmas were all around the corner.

"Let's figure this out, survive the holidays, and then we'll begin to focus on this larger case," Ava said.

"Okay, before we can stop, we have one more thing to do tonight," I said, grabbing my tote.

"Huh?" Ava looked cantankerous.

"We need to go face Denise to discuss the plan for tomorrow," I said, pushing a tired and grumpy Ava out the door.

We had the plan ready to go for the next day. Denise was extremely haughty toward Ava and me, especially since Keith had Teddy and Tabitha involved. Denise was pretty much forced into helping to find out who was behind this to save herself from jail. She had to tell Wanda about what she had done, but Teddy said she'd have to stay on at the credit union momentarily to help them nab the guy.

I dropped Ava off at her place, and Mick had come back with me. We both fell into bed with clothes on and fell straight to sleep after a long day.

I woke up the next morning to hearing someone in my kitchen. I assumed it was Ava, but then I looked next to me, and Mick wasn't there. I grabbed my pink robe with black cats all over it that Ava had bought me and plodded down the steps with Bobbi Jo and D.J. following me like baby ducklings.

Walking into the kitchen, I had déjà vu seeing my Grandma Opal and Tom Costello standing there, drinking cappuccinos and chatting with Mick. The last time this happened was the first night Mick spent with me. They had come in sporting a pineapple upside-down cake. It was somewhat embarrassing.

This morning everyone looked relaxed and like we'd been together forever—not that we'd recently patched things up for the umpteenth time.

"Hey, Grandma," I said, turning the kettle on for some hot tea. "Hi, Tom."

He raised his cup to me. "Mick makes a mean cappuccino," Tom said.

"We came to share the good news with you two love birds," Grandma said.

"What's that?" I asked, looking to see if Mick already knew, but he was shrugging his shoulders.

"Tom and I decided we are having a Christmas wedding," Grandma said.

My head snapped up in surprise. I never thought my grandma would marry again. I stood in silence.

Mick coughed and got up and leaned over Grandma, "Congratulations, you two! How wonderful," he said, hugging Grandma, then shaking Tom's hand.

Grandma looked up at me with a worried glance—which was unlike her. I shook myself out of my reverie and said, "Yeah, what is wrong with me? It's great news!"

"Oh good, because you, my dear, are my maid of honor," Grandma stated.

"Opal and I talked about it, and I think you'd make a great best man," Tom said.

Meiser and I looked shocked because Tom had family in town, and he didn't know Mick that well.

"O—o—kay," Mick dragged the word out, bewildered.

"We'll all have to sit down to make plans soon." Grandma Opal stood up, signaling to Tom that it was time to go. He obediently followed her out the door.

Mick and I looked at each other and cracked up laughing at the absurdity of it all.

Chapter Fifteen

After Tom and my grandma left, we got ready to execute our plan with Denise. While Mick was in the shower, I added a note on the I Spy Slides that Grandma had mentioned in her ten-page letter a couple of guys that Shelly had dated back in the day. One was Zacharia, who had recently done work for me, putting Mick's ramp in, then tearing it down. That is money I will never get back. Mick walked into the room, dressed but drying his thick curly hair with a towel.

"So, what exactly are you, me, and Ava doing today?" I asked him. "I know Keith is going to stake out the post office looking for someone to pick up what Denise leaves there. You said that Teddy tapped Denise's phone for the call, and Tabitha is watching her account to see if she can get an IP address when the money transfer goes through. Seems like if we can't catch him one way, we will another."

"True, but I want to be where Tabitha is to see if she can trace where the money comes from—I'm banking on it being mafia related."

"Haha," I laughed.

"What?" Mick asked, baffled.

"You're banking on it—the money transfer—good one."

"Oh, thanks." He rolled his eyes. Sometimes I felt he was more like Ava, a good friend than my boyfriend.

"What about Ava?"

"Ava said she was going to go with Keith so they could talk football and she could give him a bathroom break if needed or get food. Who knows how long they will have to wait."

"After about an hour of Ava, Keith will go nuts," I laughed.

"I guess we don't need you," Mick said with a gleam in his eye.

"Nice," I said, punching him playfully in the gut. "Hey, you're not using your cane, and your balance seems better!"

"I know. I feel pretty good, but I doubt it can work that fast. I have the cane in the living room and am going to take it with me. Also I'm still lugging that dumb wheelchair around since the doc says I never know when a relapse can take place."

I loved hearing him call the wheelchair dumb and seeing him not relying on it anymore.

"Okay, well, I'm going to go to the restaurant. Carlos is there, but I can help a little, then I'll swing by to check in on you."

"Hey, before you head out. I've been avoiding your questions about the father of Lydia's baby."

"Yeah, I noticed. She's avoided my questions too. You both should know it only makes me want to know who it is more!"

He grinned. "Honestly, Jolie, it's time you know the truth. I think Lydia and I are afraid of people knowing because she doesn't know if she wants Monty to know for fear he will grow up either following in his footsteps, or wanting to kill him."

That got the gears in my brain going. I had initially been creeped out, thinking it had to be Nestle. Then, my mind wandered to something Tonya said in the restaurant the other day.

"Hold that thought," I put a finger up to Mick and grabbed my tote for looking for my phone. "You know what, I've had to wait this long—I can wait a little longer. I have to go right now."

I think he was trying to find out what was going through my curly head, but I was out the door and hopping in my car on my way to find out the truth.

I called Ava and asked if she was with Keith.

"Yeah, why, what's up?"

"Can you get away from him momentarily without him knowing you need to so you can talk to me?"

"Um, yeah, hold on," Ava said, and she must have put her hand over the speaker because I heard her mumble to Keith asking him if he wanted anything to drink.

"Okay, I'm heading to the convenience store to grab us some Cokes."

"I need you to get Keith's phone, text Colleen asking for pictures of Ralph's body—specifically the area of bruising with the odd indention marks. Then, text them to me so I can see them. Then, obviously, delete them from his phone."

"I can't do that. If he found out, that could be construed as hindering a police investigation."

"You said Mick has offered you information. Would Keith do the same?"

"Let me call you back in a few."

I pulled into Betsy's drive and ran up and knocked.

"Jolie, hi, what a surprise," Betsy said, welcoming me inside.

"Hi, I wanted to ask you something. I saw you talking to Elijah Morrison at the festival. How do you know him?"

"He comes into my shop all the time. I didn't know that he was doing work for Mr. Nestle, though, until recently."

"How did you find that out?"

"Denise told me I had to come back into the credit union to sign some forms for the loan. I'm so happy to have someone I know and trust to take care of all this stuff financially. I guess she had me set up for a balloon payment—whatever that is. She said she had a better offer and had me come sign some paperwork. I guess that is why I was getting the calls of being behind. When I was in the credit union, Elijah and Mr. Nestle came in the office where we were and asked Denise to come out back."

"Strange," I said.

"That's what I thought."

My phone buzzed. It was Ava calling back. "Sorry, this is Ava. I'm going to step out for a second."

Betsy nodded and said, "I'll make us some iced tea and bring it to the veranda."

"Hey, what did you find out?" I asked, walking out to her deck.

"Why do you want to know?" It was Keith—that traitor!

Betsy came out but didn't have the iced tea. Her face was pale, and her eyes were enormous. She jerked her head and eyes behind her.

I put the phone down but didn't click it off. "Betsy, what's wrong? I thought you were bringing us iced tea from your kitchen."

"No time for drinks," Elijah said, pushing Betsy out onto the porch and brandishing a handgun.

"What are you doing, Elijah?" I asked. "Guns aren't your style. Poison is more your speed."

"How'd you know?" he asked, gesturing at Betsy to sit down. He pulled down the blinds Betsy had raised around the windows of her porch.

"I saw you talking to Betsy the day Ralph was poisoned. You were by her booth and by Ralph's booth at different times that day. When I met you, you shook my hand something hurt my finger. Your class ring is too big, and there's a chunk missing out of it. It left a mark on my hand. I'm assuming it will also be a match with the bruising around Ralph's rib area."

"You can't possibly know all that to be true. Besides, that's all circumstantial."

"True, but Ralph told me himself before he died."

Elijah eyed me suspiciously.

"He said what sounded like 's'mores sun' with a pause, then sun again. I thought it was 's'mores' like Betsy here's dessert, and 'sun' like the bright sun he was looking up at—saying it twice as he died. But what he was actually saying was 'Morrison's son.' You."

"He found out too much. He asked too many questions," Elijah said, staring off into nothing. Then he turned to Betsy. "And you created problems for us too."

"I have no idea what is going on. What did I do?" Betsy demanded.

"You called the credit union manager about your loan payment, sending a red flag. Now, your little gang of friends is trying to track who is behind the loans. You won't find out. You'll never figure it out," Elijah laughed.

"Wait, did Denise—" I started to ask, but Elijah cut me off. He had an insane look in his eye.

"My mom and dad have been lying to me for years. They've been faking this relationship. Meanwhile, she's out sleeping with other men. I saw her and Ralph in his car."

So, he was the one with the binoculars. I *thought* so, but he just confirmed it.

"You're so loyal to the good mayor of Tri-City. You weren't upset that Ralph may have been sleeping with your mom—you were upset that you were making big money from whoever is behind all of this for doing their dirty work—then Ralph found out and blackmailed you for twenty-five thousand dollars. But it was more than that too—it was what he knew."

"You have no clue what you are talking about!" Elijah shoved my chair back, knocking me to the floor and leaning over me, wild-eyed.

"I do. Noah isn't your father. It's John Cardinal. It's not difficult to see him in you with your strawberry-blond hair and freckles—you have the same bone structure in your face and the same smile. Noah has coal-black hair. Your mom has been working for Cardinal for a good two decades, and you're around nineteen, just starting your second year of college."

Betsy took this moment to rush toward him, but he jumped up at her, hitting her in the forehead with the butt of the gun. She fell backward to the floor. He looked around wildly, with tears springing from his eyes. A siren wailed from the front of the house and Elijah let out a squeal like a wild animal and ran out the back.

Teddy and Keith came racing in, and I pointed out back where Keith ran off. Teddy called in for an ambulance and leaned over Betsy, who was semi-conscious and moaning. She had a huge bump already forming on her head.

"Keep her awake. She may have a concussion."

I went out back to see if Keith had gotten to Elijah when Mick showed up out back, "Are you okay?" He came bounding up to me with no limp and embraced me.

"I'm fine. Betsy is the one who got hit in the head with his gun."

"How did you know it was him?" Mick asked.

"It's what you said about Monty wanting to kill his dad when he got older. Ava and I had been looking over everything the night before on the slides. It all hit me—Elijah at the festival with Betsy, by Ralph's booth, his ring that hurt me when he shook my hand, something hit my shoulder when he grabbed the money from me that day—he was always lurking with binoculars. It had to be bigger. Tonya told me she and Noah were more a couple for show than anything, and she knew John Cardinal for two decades—Elijah's age."

"That was smart, leaving the phone on. Keith patched you through, and Tabitha ran it so we all could hear. We saw no money go through Denise's account. No one called her, and even though we had her put the coupon book in the P.O. Box as instructed, no one came—then you called Ava trying to get her to get information you have no legal access to," Mick scolded.

"Hey, I didn't know that."

"Yeah, well, there's something to be said for her taking that test and understanding the lines she can and can't cross."

Keith came back through the gate, winded.

"Did you catch him?" Mick asked.

"No, I had him in my sight, then a white sedan pulled up, and he jumped in, and they took off. I didn't get a license plate number or see who it was."

"I'm betting it was mommy," I said, looking up at Mick.

"Teddy, Keith, and I thought Tonya was blackmailing Cardinal or Nestle—we had it all wrong."

"I think Elijah is in more danger from whoever is behind the loans than he is from the police," Ava said, walking out back. "I'm glad you're okay. The ambulance just took Betsy, and Teddy went with her."

Chapter Sixteen

This day already felt like several days combined into one, and it was only early afternoon. Ava and I ran back to our places to check in on the kitties, and then I went to her house to review some of the photos.

"If Tonya is the one who picked him up, then does that mean she's been in on all of it?" I wondered.

"I kind of doubt it. He's probably a mama's boy and called her when things went south."

"He wouldn't go home or to his dorm," I said, thinking about what Stella had told me earlier about her hiding spot. "Hold on."

I called Stella and asked her for directions to where she goes when she needs to get away. I wrote it all down, tried to call Mick, but got his voicemail and left a message with what I found out from Stella. Ava stood there listening as I left the voicemail, then grabbed her bag, and we headed out to see if we could find Elijah.

An hour later, I yelled at Ava, "You told me not to take my luggage bag. I had water in there. I showed you the directions when we got in your car."

We had arrived at the nature preserve outside of Tri-City and had started on the trail Stella told us about. It was getting chilly, and neither of us thought to bring a jacket or water or anything to help while being out in nature. We weren't exactly … wilderness gals. "Why would anyone design a hiking trail with a hill to walk up that is this steep?" Ava grumped as I attempted to stop hyperventilating.

I grabbed her arm, stopping not even half-way up the giant hill, then bent over with my hands on my thighs, sucking in air and wishing I had water. "What kind of question is that? It's designed for people to hike."

"Um, we can easily walk around our town—it's nice straight roads, well—except for Chesire road, which has that weird hill. I've never found out the story behind that."

"Hey, can we keep going?"

"You're the one who stopped! Also, how on earth could you have lugged around that suitcase of yours when you can't even get up this hill?" Ava turned and sat in the middle of the path, taking in a deep breath.

"What are you doing?"

"Taking in the beauty of nature all around us."

"We're not on a nature hike, and you are as winded as me. You look like you are going to vomit—just breathe. Trust me, it feels better to huff, heave, and wheeze."

Ava's brown eyes bulged as she released an enormous breath and coughed from pretending to be in shape to show me up.

"You're—" gulps of breath, chest rising and falling dramatically, "—right—air—is—good."

"How are we in our twenties and this out of shape? What are we going to be like twenty years from now?"

"Are those leaves growing in size?" Ava asked, attempting to point at branches and leaves above us.

"We've barely begun our hike, and you're delirious. Get up. Let's power through. At least coming back we'll be going downhill."

"Are you two okay?"

Ava and I almost fell over from fear.

Stella was jogging up behind us.

"What are you doing here?" I asked, stunned— not so much that she was here, but that she was jogging up the hill while speaking in a normal voice.

"You just called asking for directions, saying you were coming to check something out. It's kind of difficult to find the mini camper. I had nothing to do, so I thought I'd come to help you find it. What are you doing? You two need some alone time or something? Need to get off the beaten path for a bit?"

She seemed more chipper, which made me happy to see she was moving on from her recent trauma. I looked at Ava while gasping.

Ava filled Stella in on everything with Elijah since she was better at pretending she wasn't winded than me.

Stella's newfound happiness quickly dissolved.

"His mom was always his kryptonite. Whenever we'd all go to the camper, we all had our issues—you know how teens are—his was always his mom and her discrepancies."

"Wow, so he's known about the affairs for a while," I puffed.

"He got into gambling in high school. They had this stupid poker and Texas Holdem ring. He lost money all the time and got the crap beat out of him a few times. We stopped inviting him to go with us when he started wanting to fight some of the guys for fun while we were all trying to relax."

"I wonder if he's still gambling, and that's why he needs the money. Tonya made it seem like he was doing odds and ends jobs, but he's doing some pretty big stuff to need twenty-five grand."

"And that's the only payment we know of," Ava said, then stopped to wheeze again.

Stella looked concerned. "So, you two are going to look for him? That's what this is all about?"

"Yep," Ava said.

"How are you planning to get him to go with you?" Stella asked.

Ava and I grimaced and scratched our heads.

"I have my taser in my bag," Ava said.

"Does that knock him out completely? How will we get him to the car?" I asked.

"I don't know? I've only stunned one person, and it was not in the middle of the woods."

"We didn't think this through. We were doing so good for a while there," Ava said.

"The camper is off the trail up there." Stella pointed to a rocky path at the top of a cliff.

"How did anyone get a camper up there?" I asked, amazed. I noticed I was simultaneously sweating and freezing. Stella's makeup still looked great, she didn't have a drop of sweat on her, and her breathing was normal. Ava and I looked like a train had run over us.

"We always wondered the same thing. Someone had a theory it was a build-a-camper kit that someone put together up there," Stella said, shrugging her shoulders.

"Another mystery to solve," Ava said, looking horrified at the rocky climb ahead of us.

Stella went first and tried to help us up the rocks. She reached for me, and I reached for Ava, who grumbled the entire way.

Stella still looked stunning upon getting to the top of the cliff. Ava and I had somehow managed to get caught on multiple branches. I had burrs in my hair, and we had clothing torn with some blood showing. We were not the outdoorsy type—this was a good lesson learned.

"I swear if this punk isn't here, I'm going to kill him myself!" Ava said a little loudly.

"Who's there?" Elijah pulled back a sheet mimicking a curtain at the front window of the tiny, rusty, rickety, dirty camper.

"It's Stella, Elijah. We are worried about you."

I shoved Ava to remind her to grab her taser, still having no clue how we would get an unconscious human back down those rocks. I checked my phone. No service. Maybe we could talk him into coming with us willingly. I saw no other way around this.

"Elijah, it's Jolie. Hopefully, you realize we are concerned about your wellbeing. You held me and Betsy at gunpoint, and you hurt my friend and killed someone—yet here we are with no police. You are in danger. You've betrayed the people you work for."

"No, I did not!" he yelled out.

"That's not the way they'll see it. I think you know that, and that's why you're hiding here. You can't stay here forever," Ava called back.

"Elijah, maybe if you come with us and confess, the police will have you work with them to bring these people down. They can protect you," I said.

"In jail?" he asked doubtfully.

"Who knows? Maybe you can make a deal if you help them. Get reduced time or time served. I don't know how all of that works, but I'm sure your mom and dad will get you a top-notch attorney," I said.

Elijah opened the door, waving the gun around—not at us, but it worried me that he might do something irrational. He was laughing insanely. "My mom and my dad," he sneered. "I don't think my 'dad' will want to admit I'm his. You know he is all politics, and he'll never allow his name to be sullied."

Stella looked at him, her brows arched in a perplexed expression.

"Yeah, my mom and her affairs—you know I told you I knew she and John had been an item for a while—turns out he's my dad."

Stella's jaw dropped. "Oh, Elijah, that information right there in a good attorney's hands will make a case to explain your behavior."

I nodded in agreement, "See, between that and what you can help them with, you have a lot to work with. Now please, come with us and let us take you to Teddy in Leavensport. If there is anyone you can trust, it's him."

"And do you have anything at all to drink in there before we go?" Ava asked.

I elbowed her in the side, "What? I'm dying here!"

"Okay, I guess. I want to call my mom when we get to a place with reception," Elijah said, looking at the gun.

"Why don't you leave that," I said. "You can use my phone if you need it."

Elijah looked at me suspiciously and walked to the edge of the cliff, looking over it. My stomach dropped. He had the gun in hand and was hesitating for too long.

"Elijah," Stella said, walking toward him. I reached out to grab her, but she shook me off.

He turned, then tossed the gun over the cliff, then looked back at the three of us. "I do know a lot. Not everything, but enough," he finally said.

Stella ran up and hugged him when a loud shot rang out. Ava and I jumped, looking in the direction confused. A figure erupted from the bush below and sprinted down the path away from us.

Everything happened so fast. I turned to look and saw Elijah with blood running from his back. I couldn't tell if Stella or Elijah or both were hit.

"Stella," I screamed, running toward her as Elijah fell back with Stella in his arms.

"NO!" Ava dashed after me.

I grabbed at Stella's sweatshirt hood and pulled back hard. That caused Elijah to loosen his grip on Stella, and he fell over the cliff. Stella stumbled, and she found herself intertwined with him. Me grabbing her hood and him falling caused her to twist her body around, and she grabbed the edge, wild-eyed, screaming in fear. Elijah's scream rang out as he fell.

Ava threw herself to the ground, gripping Stella's arm. I held the hood with one hand and held onto her other arm.

"We've got you," I heard myself say firmly as I stared her straight in the eye. How was my voice so calm when my entire body felt like flames were burning me from the inside out?

Stella was writhing in panic so much that we were struggling to keep a grip on her.

"Hold on to us," Ava said. "Stop kicking."

"Stella, we aren't letting you go," I said, nodding for her to trust me. "Think back to Pria helping you climb that rope. You've got this. Trust us."

She turned her neck slowly, looking down, closed her eyes and gulped.

"I got her," Teddy yelled, leaning over us and grabbing under her arms, lifting as Ava and I held on to each arm.

Stella stumbled to the ground, breathing similarly to how Ava and I were earlier. I felt around her back, pulling the hoodie off. "Were you hit?"

I went from calm and confident to panic in two point five seconds.

"I don't—I don't—think—so—maybe," Stella looked at her body as tears poured out, then she crawled away from us and vomited.

I didn't blame her.

"What were you two thinking!" Teddy yelled. It was a question phrased as a punishment.

"We reacted without a lot of thought," I said, walking to Stella and rubbing her back, partly to comfort her and partly to feel for any wounds.

"We need to see if she was shot. Yell at us later," Ava huffed, grabbing the sweatshirt and pulling it off.

We saw Stella's T-shirt wet with blood, but she lifted it. Teddy respectfully turned away as we checked her torso.

"I think the blood is all from Elijah," I said, realizing the adrenaline had gotten the best of all of us.

"Elijah," Stella said softly.

"Let's get you all to safe ground, and then you need to give a report of everything that happened."

"Stella gets checked out first," I said.

"Of course," Teddy said.

Chapter Seventeen

Saturday, September 19, 2020

"He was dead. No one could find any wounds on his body. Meanwhile, she was having the baby at the exact same time at the festival—you already know all of this!" I raised my voice as I sat across from the brown eyes I knew so well. The ones I grownto love over the last two years.

Except I was looking at harder, colder eyes through the plexiglass between me and Mick's brother, Marty Milano.

It had been a long two weeks, and yesterday alone felt like a full month. The staff at the hospital checked Stella, and she was fine, at least physically. I'm not sure she'll ever go back what was her safe spot again. I told Stella she ought to talk to someone about her traumatic experience and recommended Tabitha to her.

No one knew who shot Elijah at this point, but Teddy, Mick, and Keith were working with Tri-City detectives to look into it. Speaking of Mick, he was less than thrilled with my hijinks, but even though I was so tired I wanted to sleep for a year straight, we stayed up last night and talked about everything that happened. He told me that Marty had a one-night stand with Lydia last Thanksgiving, and

Monty was conceived. That was why Lydia didn't want anyone to know—I have to admit I was relieved it was Marty over Nestle. It suddenly made sense that Meiser was so keen on protecting her and being there for her. He felt a responsibility for her since it was his criminal of a brother who knocked her up. Plus, he was related to Monty and had told her how his great-grandfather was one of the only decent people he knew from his family. I was having a difficult time disliking Lydia now.

Mick was here with me, but standing out of sight from his brother after the situation with them last November. Ava was sitting next to me.

"I have a right to know my son," Marty said through the phone he held up to his ear.

"No, when you tried to kill your brother, you lost that right," I said.

"You have no idea what you've gotten yourself into when you hooked up with my brother. This is bigger than either of you could ever imagine," he grinned.

"Why are you taking the blame for Elijah?" Ava asked. She and I were sharing the phone.

"I put a hit on him. It's what we in the mafia do." Marty shrugged like it was nothing.

"No one believes you put a hit on him. We're looking into who is behind it," Mick said, stepping out where Marty could see him.

It was the first time I'd ever seen Marty look nervous. That calm, cocky demeanor melted away as he faced his brother who in his eyes had betrayed his family.

"It doesn't matter. I'm happy to tell you, big brother, who I hired to do the killing," Marty's demeanor switched back to brash, and he sat back.

"Okay, who?" Meiser said into the phone. It was getting difficult for three to share one phone.

"Easy, his dad," Marty grinned.

"Mayor Cardinal?!?" Ava and I shrieked in unison.

"No, the pretend dad—Noah. He's a great fall guy to protect all who need protected in our little web," Marty's eyes gleamed as he hung up the phone, satisfied with our expressions.

Mick turned around and went for the door to go up front to call Teddy. Ava and I stared open-mouthed at each other.

Chapter Eighteen

Grandma Opal threw a giant shindig to celebrate her engagement to Tom Costello, Leavensport's local grocer. She set it up to begin at the community center, which was large enough to house the entire Tucker family as well as most of the Leavensport villagers. Baggy and Myrtle were vying for the best position to perform to the residents of Leavensport. I felt a rivalry coming on. I thought they were only performing for the festival, but it was looking more and more like we had ourselves a permanent troubadour with a doggy side-kick and a jazz-singing performance artist. Oddly, they fit well into our quirky little hamlet.

I never figured out the beef between my two uncles, but for today, at least, everyone seemed to be being civil. I noticed the uncles were staying on opposite sides of the community center, though.

Ava had been acting odd the whole morning before the engagement party, but when I tried prying what was going on out of her, she refused to answer.

I was getting more snacks for the partygoers from the kitchen of the community center. Grandma Opal had reserved a room at M&M's Italian restaurant for an after-the-engagement party-party. Leave it to my family to plan a party for a party on the same afternoon. While I was tempted to eat the salmon puffs I had made, I resisted, knowing we would all be eating at Mick's place soon. My mind began to wander over everything I had found out recently.

Mick, Teddy, Keith, and Tabitha had followed up on the information about Noah that Marty had provided. It panned out a little too easily if you ask me. He seemed more than willing to be the fall guy, readily admitting to shooting Elijah, the rifle with a telescope was in plain sight with his prints on it when they went to his house to confront him. Tabitha tried to get him to deal for lesser time, but he refused. A few days later, we heard he was attacked and killed in jail while awaiting trial. Yet again, we couldn't connect anything to Nestle or Mayor Cardinal, just like Elijah predicted.

Stella, Peggy, and Gemma had let us know that many people in the city were in an uproar with what happened in our town and how Ava and I had handled things with Elijah. Mayor Cardinal had held several press conferences that appeared to be heartfelt and offer condolences to the bereaved but had an undertone that seemed to blame the village and our PI services in particular for the tragic outcome. They warned that we might want to watch ourselves as they felt like there was a rivalry brewing among urbanites against the villagers. I wondered if the mayor was doing this on purpose to see if he could drive the price of the land down. I wouldn't put it past him to start a war to save himself money and gain him more fame.

Stella was looking to close down the pizza shop in Tri-City and move it to Leavensport—another thing that angered many in the city. She wanted to change the name to Ralph & Stella's NY Pizza Pie. I was all for it!

I robotically carried snacks around like a waitress to the guests while pondering the chaos that is my life. Many people had begun heading out after congratulating the happy couple and wolfing down the food. The Tucker family was getting ready to head to M&M's Italian restaurant for dinner. A few of Grandma's friends offered to stay at the community center on clean-up duty, which we all appreciated.

Upon everyone arriving at M&M's and beginning to take their seats, Ava stood and clinked a glass. "Can I get everyone's attention for a moment, please?"

She looked ready to puke. Everyone quieted down as Ava pulled something out of her pocket, knelt on one knee, and flipped open the navy satin box to reveal a beautiful diamond ring. "Delilah, you've stood by me at the best and worst of times. I can't imagine life without you in it. Will you do me the honor of marrying me?"

My hands flew to my mouth in excitement as Mick wrapped his arms around me, leaning into my neck and breathing in my hair.

Delilah looked equally excited and emotional as she blurted out, "YES!" Everyone clapped as the two embraced.

"Oh my gosh, we should do a double ceremony," Grandma Opal squealed in glee.

I grimaced, "Grandma–" I started.

"Mawmaw Opal, I hope I didn't steal your thunder," Ava said.

"Child, I'm an old woman. I'm tickled for the two of you!"

I noticed my Uncle Eddie and Uncle Wylie looked to be having a heated conversation and began to inch closer to them. Shelly looked very uncomfortable sitting at the table by them.

"Hey, you two, no one knows what's going on, but maybe you could hold off on the family argument for just today," I said with arms crossed.

My mom had been thinking the same as me and came up and put a hand on my back. "Guys, seriously, can you at least take it outside?"

My Uncle Wylie, always the jovial one, had a stern look on his face and pointed to the door to the patio, signaling Uncle Eddie to follow him.

Mom and I looked at each other nervously, and then Shelly stood up to follow them outside.

"What is going on with them? Do you know the story?" I asked my mom.

"All the adults know," my mom said.

"Um, hello," I gestured theatrically up and down my body. "I'm an adult now. I'd like to know what is happening with our family."

"It's complicated," Mom said.

"Isn't it always?"

Mom took a deep breath in and exhaled slowly, looked around the room, grabbed my elbow, and led me to a corner booth for some privacy. Maybe I didn't want to know.

"When we were all in high school, your Uncle Wylie dated Shelly. It was always an off-and-on sort of relationship. I don't think anyone thought too much about that since they were so young," Mom started.

What? Uncle Wylie dated Shelly? I couldn't imagine that. I thought about what that said for

Meiser and me and our off-again-on-again relationship.

"Later, I found out that Shelly had always been interested in Eddie. What I didn't know was that Eddie felt the same about her."

"Yikes," I said, biting my lower lip.

"Exactly. Right after we graduated, Wylie and Shelly were an item again. Wylie asked her to marry him, and she told him she needed time to think about it."

"Why on earth would she do that when she loved someone else?"

"I think she truly cared for Wylie, and she was young and confused. What I didn't know at the time was that she was pregnant with twins. No one knew then."

"Karly and Kevin?" I asked, knowing they were older than the other three kids. Suddenly it all fell into place.

Mom nodded.

"Wait, so they are—"

"They are your Uncle Wylie's kids, Jolie. Shelly loved Eddie. She went to him and told him everything. Eddie, being young and in love, proposed to her. The two of them took off and got married without telling anyone. No one in the family heard from them."

"What about Uncle Wylie?"

"Shelly left him a Dear John letter. She never told him she was pregnant. Only how sorry she was that she didn't feel the same about him."

"Wow, no wonder there is bad blood there," I said, shaking my head slowly in disbelief.

"Your grandmother went ballistic. You know how she gets. She takes sides. She sided with Uncle Wylie and pretty much decided to disown Eddie. That didn't help matters any."

"But, didn't Uncle Wylie want to see his kids? I can't believe he wouldn't want to be a part of their lives?"

"He never knew they were his until recently. I think that with time, they could have forgiven each other. But finding out about the kids has really taken a toll on everyone in the family. That's why when Tink came here everything was so tense and awkward."

"And it's why the last several months have been stranger than ever with the family," I said, thinking back to everything—all the evasion, Cheerful Uncle Wylie suddenly grim, all the awkwardness.

"The two of them need to work through this. At least they are thinking about the kids," Mom said.

"They're adults now, too, though," I said, thinking about the fact that Karly and Kevin were only a couple years older than me.

"You know what I mean. Those two, or three with Shelly, need to work things out between them before they move forward."

"You mean Kevin and Karly don't know!?" I yelled, then immediately slapped my hand over my mouth, looking around, wide-eyed. Thank goodness it was loud enough no one seemed to notice.

"No, they don't, and you don't need to say a thing to anyone. Not Ava, not Mick—no one, Jolie. This is important. They need to figure out how they want to do this, not us."

I nodded.

Chapter Nineteen

Friday, October 2, 2020

It's hard to believe a month has come and gone, and all that has taken place in a short amount of time. My heart still aches for my cousins and my uncles, and for Aunt Shelly too. As far as I know, nothing has been resolved there, and the holiday season is right around the corner. A huge part of me wishes that they would just get it all out in the open so the family can feud and then begin to heal, while another part hopes they wait until after the holidays, especially with Grandma Opal and Ava's weddings coming up this December.

Recently, I found out that Bradley started dating Gemma. That was at least some good news. I guess Lahiri and Bradley are working on a story for The Village Herald. Bradley is looking into information about scandals on Tri-City college campuses, and supposedly Lahiri has information? I told him I wasn't sure I'd trust her. I heard that child went from blaming her Uncle Nalini for stealing her "clubbing" money to then blaming the maid, all to find out, she was fibbing to get more money. I feel like a jerk, but since I'm journaling here and no one else gets to read this, I'll just say, it's nice to see other people screw up more than me.

Ugh, and poor Keith. His sister, Denise, was fired from the credit union. We all knew that was coming. Next, Teddy had no choice but to officially charge her for her part in scheming people out of money and creating false loans—Tabitha made sure of it since it was federal, and she's with the FBI. She was charged and sentenced and spent a few weeks in jail while Keith took care of the kids. The judge went light on her because she attempted to aid the police in finding the person behind it. Currently, she's on parole and doing community service. She still does not have official custody of her kids, and I heard her ex is sniffing around threatening to try and get full custody of them. Keith is going to try to intervene, last I heard.

Mick is doing fantastic. Regardless of all the insanity that is going on with my family, Keith's family, and two weddings coming up with the holidays, the new medication is working. He hasn't used a wheelchair once in two full weeks. His balance still is a little off from time to time, but it's like Dr. Delagada said, it's his new normal. His mood has improved drastically, and he's back working with Teddy full-time starting Monday. He hired Denise as a part-time waitress and is working with her parole officer. I'm so proud of him for facing everything he has this last year. Also, I know it can't be easy for him to reach out and do anything for Keith, knowing our history, but it makes me so grateful because I know he's doing it because he finally has complete faith in what we have together—as do I.

Time will tell what happens with the families in Leavensport. The holidays and two weddings all within the span of one month—what could go wrong?

Recipes

Cast Iron Skillet Deep Dish Pizza
taken and adjusted slightly from
https://minimalistbaker.com/simple-deep-dish-pizza/

Ingredients
- 1/2 batch pizza dough recipe (or sub store-bought)
- 1/2 cup pizza sauce
- 1 cup mixed veggies of choice (such as cherry tomatoes, eggplant, onion, green pepper, mushroom)
- Olive oil
- 1 clove garlic
- 1/2 cup mozzarella cheese
- Italian seasonings (dried basil, oregano, thyme, red pepper, etc. // *optional*)
- Grated parmesan cheese (*optional*)
- Fresh basil (*optional*)

Instructions
1. Prepare pizza dough and sauce if using homemade.

2. If roasting veggies, preheat oven to broil, toss veggies in olive oil on a baking sheet, and broil for 4-6 minutes on the top rack (low/medium broil), tossing once for even cooking. Or if using a parchment-lined baking sheet, roast veggies at 450 degrees F as the broiling function is unsafe with parchment paper. Remove from oven and set aside.

3. Preheat oven to 450 degrees F

4.Next, coat a cast-iron skillet or round baking dish with olive oil and run a garlic clove around for seasoning. Plop your dough down into the pan and push it up around the sides about 1 to 1.5 inches (see photo). Let rest for a few minutes while preparing the rest of your toppings.

5.First, sprinkle in 1/2 of mozzarella cheese, then add veggies, then sauce. Top with remaining mozzarella cheese, Italian seasonings (dried basil, oregano, thyme, red pepper, etc.) and grated parmesan cheese.

6.Bake for 25-30 minutes or until the crust is golden brown and the cheese and sauce are bubbly. Let rest for 5-10 minutes before cutting, then serve immediately.

Poblano Stuffed Pepper
taken and adjusted slightly from:
https://www.southerncastiron.com/stuffed-poblano-peppers/

Ingredients

- 3 large poblano peppers, halved and seeded
- ½ cup yellow corn kernels
- ½ cup chopped red onion
- 1 tablespoon olive oil
- 2 cloves garlic, minced
- 1 plum tomato, diced
- ½ cup long-grain rice, cooked
- ½ cup canned black beans, drained and rinsed
- ½ cup cubed Monterey Jack cheese with peppers
- ½ cup chopped fresh cilantro
- ½ teaspoon kosher salt
- ½ teaspoon ground cumin
- 2 tablespoons crumbled goat cheese
- Garnish: chopped fresh cilantro

Instructions

1. Preheat oven to broil.

2. Heat a 12-inch cast-iron skillet over high heat. Add poblanos; cook, turning frequently, until charred on all sides, about 5 minutes. Remove from skillet. Add corn and onion; cook, stirring occasionally, until charred, about 3 minutes. Add oil and garlic; cook until garlic is fragrant, about 1 minute.

3. In a large bowl, stir together corn mixture, tomatoes, cooked rice, beans, Monterey Jack,

cilantro, salt, and cumin until combined. Place charred peppers in skillet. Spoon corn mixture into pepper halves. Sprinkle with goat cheese.

4. Broil until cheese is melted, 2 to 3 minutes. Garnish with cilantro, if desired.

Fried Chicken with Wilted Bok Choy

taken and slightly adjusted from:
https://www.bonappetit.com/recipe/skillet-fried-chicken

Ingredients

- 2 tablespoons kosher salt, divided
- 2 teaspoons plus 1 tablespoon freshly ground black pepper
- 1 1/2 teaspoons paprika
- 3/4 teaspoon cayenne pepper
- 1/2 teaspoon garlic powder
- 1/2 teaspoon onion powder
- 1 3–4-lb. chicken (not kosher), cut into 10 pieces, backbone and wing tips removed
- 1 cup buttermilk
- 1 large egg
- 3 cups all-purpose flour
- 1 tablespoon cornstarch
- Peanut oil (for frying)

Instructions

1. Whisk 1 Tbsp. salt, 2 tsp. black pepper, paprika, cayenne, garlic powder, and onion powder in a small bowl. Season chicken with spices. Place chicken in a medium bowl, cover, and chill overnight.
2. Let chicken stand covered at room temperature for 1 hour. Whisk buttermilk, egg, and 1/2 cup water in a medium bowl. Whisk flour, cornstarch, remaining 1 Tbsp.

salt, and remaining 1 Tbsp. pepper in a 9x13x2" baking dish.

3. Pour oil into a 10"–12" cast-iron skillet or other heavy straight-sided skillet (not nonstick) to a depth of 3/4". Prop deep-fry thermometer in oil so bulb is submerged. Heat over medium-high heat until thermometer registers 350°. Meanwhile, set a wire rack inside a large rimmed baking sheet.

4. Working with 1 piece at a time (use 1 hand for wet ingredients and the other for dry ingredients), dip chicken in buttermilk mixture, allowing excess to drip back into bowl. Dredge in flour mixture; tap against bowl to shake off excess. Place 5 pieces of chicken in skillet. Fry chicken, turning with tongs every 1–2 minutes and adjusting heat to maintain a steady temperature of 300°– 325°, until skin is deep golden brown and an instant-read thermometer inserted into thickest part of chicken registers 165°, about 10 minutes for wings and 12 minutes for thighs, legs, and breasts.

5. Using tongs, remove chicken from skillet, allowing excess oil to drip back into skillet; transfer chicken to prepared rack.

6. Repeat with remaining chicken pieces; let cool for at least 10 minutes before serving.

Wilted Bok Choy

This is a recipe I've created from trying multiple versions from about seven recipes and found this to have the BEST flavor!

Ingredients
- 1 tbsp. vegetable oil
- 3 tbsp. butter
- 2 tbsp. hoisin sauce
- 1 tbsp. chopped peeled fresh ginger
- 3 heads baby bok choy, sliced
- Hot sesame oil, for drizzling

Instructions
In cast-iron skillet, add butter, hoisin, and ginger. In skillet, cook bok choy over medium-high, stirring, for 4 minutes, season. Serve with bok choy. Drizzle bok choy with hot sesame oil.

S'more dessert
taken directly from:
https://www.foodnetwork.com/recipes/ayesha-curry/skillet-smores-3513346

Ingredients
- 1 1/2 cups semisweet chocolate chips
- 1 1/2 cups butterscotch chips
- 1/4 cup heavy cream
- 3 cups mini marshmallows
- Graham crackers, broken into squares, for serving
-

Instructions
1.Place an oven rack in the top position and preheat the oven to 450 degrees F. While the oven heats, put a 10-inch cast-iron or stainless-steel skillet in to heat.

2.Carefully remove the hot skillet and sprinkle the chocolate and butterscotch chips in the bottom. Drizzle the cream over the top and then top with the marshmallows in an even layer. Set the skillet on the top oven rack and bake until the marshmallows are molten and golden on top, 5 to 6 minutes.

3.Serve (carefully, the pan will be very hot) with graham crackers for dipping.

Carlos' Heavens to Murgatroyd Cast Iron Queso

taken and adjusted slightly from:
https://www.rachaelraymag.com/recipe/loaded-queso-fundido

Ingredients

- 1 pound pepper jack, shredded
- 1 pound American cheese, shredded
- 1 chipotle in adobo sauce, minced, plus 1 tbsp. sauce
- Toppings: crumbled cooked fresh chorizo, sliced scallions, diced tomatoes, sliced jalapenos, sliced radishes, fresh cilantro leaves
- Tortilla chips, for dipping

Instructions

Preheat the oven to 400 degrees . In a large bowl, mix the cheeses, minced chipotle and adobo sauce. Transfer to a medium cast-iron or other ovenproof skillet, spreading in an even layer. Bake until the cheese melts, bubbles and browns in spots, 15 to 20 minutes. Garnish with toppings. Serve with the chi

Carlos' Zoinks! Tex Mex Skillet Pie
taken and adjusted slightly from:
https://www.rachaelraymag.com/recipe/tex-mex-skillet-pie

Ingredients
- 1 package (8.5 oz.) corn muffin mix
- 1/3 cup milk
- 1 egg
- 1 tablespoon minced seeded jalapeno
- 1 tablespoon plus 1 1/2 tsp. canola oil
- 3/4 pound sweet potatoes, peeled and cut into 1/3-inch cubes
- 1 medium red onion, chopped
- 1/2 lb. boneless beef chuck, cut into 1/2-inch cubes
- 1 can (14.5 oz.) diced tomatoes with juices
- 1 cup drained canned corn
- 1 cup chopped fresh cilantro
- 1 small canned chipotle in adobo, minced, plus 2 tsp. adobo sauce

Instructions
1.Preheat the oven to 425 degrees . In a large bowl, stir the corn muffin mix, milk, egg and jalapeno until just combined.

2.Brush the bottom and sides of a large cast-iron skillet with 1 tbsp. oil; heat over high. Add the sweet potatoes and onion; season with salt and pepper. Cook, stirring often, until the vegetables soften, about 3 minutes; transfer to a medium bowl.

3.In the same skillet, heat the remaining 1 1/2 tsp. oil over medium-high. Add the beef, season and cook until browned, about 3 minutes. Off heat, stir in the tomatoes and their juices, the corn, cilantro, chipotle, adobo sauce and the sweet potato mixture; season.

4.Spread the mixture evenly in the skillet; top with the muffin batter, leaving a 2-inch border. Bake until the cornbread is golden and a tester inserted in its center comes out clean, 15 to 18 minutes.

From the Author

I'm finding in continuing to write this series that I'm digging into more and more research on many different topics. This book was no different. I found myself researching topics from poisons to MS symptoms and treatments to ways to smuggle diamonds into small towns to mafia activity.

Please note if you are an expert on any topics that I ever research, and if you find mistakes, I have been an educator going on close to twenty-five years now, but more importantly, I'm a life-long learner. Any mistakes found in any of these books in this series are solely mine. I would love to know if you find anything or if you have more knowledge on a topic than I do--feel free to email me at jrath@columbus.rr.com.

Exciting News

***A percentage of all purchases from every book in The Cast Iron Skillet Mystery Series will be donated to the following two organizations: The MS Society and TrueColors United! Thank you for helping those that live with MS and homeless youth! For more information about those navigating life with MS, please visit The MS Society's page at https://www.nationalmssociety.org/ For more information about homeless teens, please visit True Colors United page at https://truecolorsunited.org/

Yuletide Cast of the Iron Skillet Blurb

Welcome to Leavensport, OH, where *DEATH* takes a *DELICIOUS* turn!

Holiday folly—LITERALLY! Alongside a murder comes another new little addition to the human race in Leavensport, Ohio. Not to mention a broken-off engagement, a double wedding, and buried bones in the village chapel cellar. The Martinez family is back in town to observe Nochebuena with Ava as the Tucker family gears up for their Christmas feast. Leavensport community center is abuzz with preparations for the village multi-cultural shindig until the discovery of an old unresolved crime casts a dark shadow over the town. Will Jolie and Ava solve their first cold case in time to save the holiday celebrations—and will they both survive it?

Read on for a Sneak Peek at Chapter One of *Yuletide Cast of the Iron Skillet*, which comes out December 18, 2020.

Chapter One

I loved the winter season—snow blanketed the ground and snowflakes fell from the pastel sky as the sun began to set behind the puffy clouds. I was cozy in a fluffy, warm coat, mittens, a hat, a scarf, boots, and a sweater. I had hot cocoa in one hand, and my other hand was holding tall, dark-haired Mick's, making his brown eyes gleam with joy. This was our first Christmas together in the village. Every year, I picked an evening and enjoyed taking a long, leisurely walk right at twilight when the lights came on, starting in the southeast corner of the village and slowly working my way around Leavensport.

"I appreciate you allowing me to horn in on your loner time." Mick squeezed my hand tighter.

"I'm getting used to not being alone so much. Plus, it's fun to get to show you everything and talk to someone while doing my annual walk."

I met him at his Italian restaurant, M&M's, since it was right at the southeast corner, and he had large to-go mugs of steaming hot cocoa with marshmallows in them. I was giddier and more excited to start a new tradition with Mick than our upcoming Christmas holiday because this was something that was all ours.

"I think you and Ava went a tad overboard with decorations on my place," Mick said, standing out in front of the restaurant with his phone ready to snap a picture of the large pine he had in front of the restaurant. We had hung green, white, and red ornaments all over it and draped ribbons around the boughs that represented the Italian flag. A huge lily sat on top of the pine—the official Italian flower. "You know it's my family that was born in Italy, not me, right?"

"Hey, this was all Ava's idea. She thought it would be a cute theme considering you serve Italian food. I was opposed to doing branding for your restaurant. Personally, I think you should pay us, as we are helping you to beef up your business," I gave him a playful shrug with my pink mittens that had black cats on them then sipped my rich, chocolatey cocoa.

He grabbed me around the waist of my puffy black coat and pulled me into his buttoned-up, wool jacket nuzzling my blonde, curly hair, "You just let me know what type of payment you'll take."

"I take all sorts of payments," I said, reaching up for a light kiss while feeling my heart flutter. "Now, enough of this, it's time to take a stroll."

We sauntered north moving next door to the Make Yourself at Home B&B. "Every year, there are certain places in the village that work to honor as many December cultures and religions as possible, and the B&B is one of them. I love that many of our villagers came to live here from all around the world. Regardless of how gossipy and judgmental some of the villagers can be at times, the majority of us attempt to understand people of different cultures than our own. My family worked to teach me this growing up, and our teachers did a great job as well. I had different teachers from different cultures."

"That's pretty amazing. Most small villages have little to no diversity."

"I know, and I've never really understood how that happened, but I'm thankful for it. It's one of the reasons I love starting my walk here because the B&B is so large and the owners do such a great job of blending cultural decorations with the reds and greens for Christmas, the orange, greens, yellow, and black for Kwanzaa, and the Jewish blue and white for Hanukkah."

"I imagine they have many families from all over who come to stay here around this time to be with those that live here in the town," Mick said.

I nodded, taking another sip of my cocoa and slurping up a marshmallow that had melted, savoring the soft vanilla flavor mixed with chocolate.

As we walked through the park, I noticed the gazebo covered in puffy, white snow and said more to myself than Mick, "It would have been nice to see a wedding in the gazebo."

I was referring to the upcoming double wedding with my grandma and local grocer Tom Costello and my best friend, Ava, and her girlfriend, Delilah.

"I'm sure the church will look beautiful, too."

I thought Ava was going to be the bridezilla, but it was Grandma Opal who was pushing Tom's wallet to the limit. According to my mom, Grandma's wedding with Grandpa all those years ago was rather underwhelming.

The park was a winter wonderland, with a ton of blues and whites everywhere. We continued to walk through their path, enjoying the inflatable snowmen and women, Santa and Mrs. Claus, and the reindeer. Out of nowhere, the decorations seemed to take a eerie turn. We came across a horned figure that looked like he was leftover from Halloween, and an impish-looking creature standing next to him.

"Um, am I missing something here?" I looked up at Mick.

"That's Krampus and Belsnickel, and over there is Gryla! NO! Is that really Ded Moroz? I've only seen pictures." Mick raced toward a man that resembled Santa Claus, except he was bent over with a cane or stick of some sort, carrying an old rustic bag of what looked to be gifts over his shoulder. The man carried a pipe with slash marks on his hand.

"I'm sorry, but did you just say dead moron? Who on earth celebrates dead morons?" I asked incredulously.

I'm not sure what the look on my face was, but Mick turned to me, grinned, then bent over with a hearty laugh.

"What's so funny? You're the one who said it!"

"Ded Mor*oz*," Meiser said, emphasizing the last syllable. "He's similar to Santa, but he's Slavic, and he normally has a family member with him who is called a Snow Maiden, or something. I can't remember her name now."

"Probably something like 'Snow Wench,' based on this dude's name," I said, scrunching my eyebrows in contemplation.

"Hey, you were the one who was just preaching celebrating the diversity of cultures and traditions," he teased.

"Yeah, yeah, I suck. I guess I'm just used to bubbly, cheerful holiday lore."

"You do this stroll annually. Is this the first time you've seen these characters?" Mick asked.

"What are you two up to?" someone called from behind us.

I turned to see Lydia bundled in a cute purple wool Paddington coat with red mittens and matching scarf and earmuffs. Baby Monty, now three months old, was in a stroller with a blanket over him so that we couldn't see his face.

"I'm doing my stroll through the town but decided not to trek it alone this year and brought this guy with me," I said, slugging Mick in the bicep.

"Not the loner anymore," Lydia said, pulling back the blanket and taking her gloves off to touch Monty's cheek. Being childless, I assumed she was checking his body temperature. He was bundled up in a padded little blue and yellow snowsuit with a hood covering his head and ears. He was wriggling around in his suit happily with drool coming out of his mouth.

"I'm not a loner," I protested while bending over the buggy, blowing out my cheeks and widening my eyes at Monty and waving to him. "He's giggling at me!"

"That's got to be gas," Mick said wryly. "No one could possibly find you funny."

"Jerk," I slapped his stomach, feeling his six-pack underneath the coat and shirt. Mick has MS, and he went through a trial and switched medicines earlier in the year. Since then, the balance issues he was having, including momentarily putting him in a wheelchair, have straightened out, and he's been working out a lot more. I wasn't complaining!

Except for the feeling of guilt for my lack of rippling abs.

"Sorry, Jolie, he's right, it is gas." Lydia giggled, and her green eyes lit up. "I'm happy you two found each other. I was kidding about the loner comment—kind of. You've always been quiet and kept more to yourself than others—at least around me."

I grinned at her. Lydia and I had a past rivalry that recently took a turn for a more harmonious relationship. "I don't remember you sharing your deepest secrets with me either," I teased back.

"Well, we should do a girls' night sometime," Lydia said. "If only I could find a babysitter ..." She looked sideways at Meiser.

"How about Uncle Mick?" Meiser said, reaching down to place a hand on Monty and rubbing his little belly as the baby wiggled his arms.

"Sounds great!" Lydia and I said in unison.

"You two call each other and make all your plans and just let me know," he said, waving at Monty.

"You're nice," I said, leaning up on tiptoes to kiss him as Lydia pushed the baby carriage beyond us.

"I'd love to spend some time with the little guy." Mick wrapped his arms around me.

"We need to quit stopping for so many kisses, or we'll be out here all night."

"You," I said, flirtatiously, running a few fingers up his chest to bop him on his nose, "are right. Let's go." I dropped my empty cocoa cup into a nearby trashcan.

"You're good with kids." Mick reached for my hand.

"Really? I feel so weird with babies. I think it's 'only child syndrome.'"

"Did you babysit?"

"Nope, never did. I haven't been around too many babies, and Lydia is the first in the group we hang out with from graduation to have a baby." I looked up at his face trying to see more. "I know we talked about this before, but let me do another *check-in* as Tabitha calls them—You do still want kids, don't you?"

"I want you," he said, lifting my mittened hand kissing it as we continued our stroll past the bank, the Leavensport Lion's school district, and walked in quietude as we moved south past the mall taking in the light display in the circle in the middle of our quaint town.

We stopped at the end of the street to turn around and see the piles of snow that were pushed to the side in huge drifts from the snow plows with different colored lights displayed on every building left to right with reds, greens, purples, pinks, and blues standing out and shining the brightest. The village looked beautiful, with the bare trees lining the streets with lights draped through the branches, and large snowflake lights spread out throughout the branches of each tree in blue lights. There was a huge pine in the center of town that we all decorated every year. That was coming up this weekend, and I couldn't wait!

I took a deep breath in and breathed out, "So, aren't you going to *check in* with me and ask me if I want kids or not?"

"We said we'd go our own pace and see where we ended up," he said, steering us into Chocolate Capers, where our friend Betsy owned and ran the shop.

"Wait, we're not finished," I said, pulling him back.

"I know. We're out of hot chocolate, and where else has better cocoa than Chocolate Capers?"

"Good point." I pointed to him and pushed past him, taking my mittens off.

"Hey, guys, what are you up to?" Betsy's long red hair was in two braids dangling to each shoulder. She wore a green Christmas sweater that read "Merry Woofmas" and had a bulldog on the front. Betsy had a bulldog named Biscuit that had a big personality. I swore he was more human than dog. He seemed to understand everything Betsy said.

"I'm taking Meiser on a walk through the village to see all the lights and decorations. We ran out of hot cocoa, though," I said, looking around the shop. "OOOoooo, you got a fish tank!"

Betsy laughed, "I did. I spent some time researching it before I did so I know how to care for them and keep the tank clean. I thought it would be fun to have them here since I'm here so much. I was hoping the patrons would enjoy them too."

"Good call, obviously this one is enjoying them," Mick said, pulling out his wallet to pay for our hot beverages.

"Oh, I knew she'd squeal as soon as she saw them." Betsy rang us up and handed him the change.

I walked back and tapped the glass. "Hi guys, how's it going? Oh, you are a Beatrice—no doubt in my mind, and you look just like a guy from high school, Calvin." I turned to Betsy and called, "Do you remember Calvin? Whatever happened to him? This guy looks like Calvin, right?"

Mick and Betsy had an odd stare, but neither looked completely surprised. I was known to have full blown conversations with my cats and had the cats talk back to me. I was positive I knew what they would say in return. Also, no one would put it past me to talk to inanimate objects as well.

"Not sure what happened to good ole' Calvin, but sure, let's name those two Calvin and Beatrice. Also, I need to put a sign up that says, 'please don't tap on the glass.'" Betsy looked at Meiser playfully and laughed.

"I'll take her off your hands," Mick said, pulling me from the fish tank.

"See you two soon," Betsy said, grabbing for a piece of paper and marker to make her sign to ward off the crazies like me that would be tempted to tap at and talk to the fish.

We moved southwest, beyond some of the farmland at the edge of town, and I pointed toward the Grubers' home, where they always had the best Hanukkah decorations every year. "Have you met the Gruber family? I always love to look at their place. Every year they change it up."

Two eight-foot, white, wicker bears stood with blue sweaters and hats, holding a white-lighted sign that said 'Happy Hanukkah,' and they had some large, illuminated dreidels off to the side of the yard.

"I don't remember meeting them, but maybe. Yeah, they go all out!" Mick took a picture of their yard.

"Huh, that's odd–their eldest daughter, Rachel, is a friend who has shared a lot about the Jewish faith with me. She's seen you around town. She's infatuated with you." I grinned at him.

His cheeks turned two shades of red as he shook his head, "You'll have to point her out so I can steer clear then."

"Oh, I will," I said, grabbing his arm possessively. "So, I wanted to throw this out there," I said, licking my lips and looking away, butterflies fluttering in my stomach.

"What's that?"

"Tabitha suggested maybe we try couples counseling." Now I was biting my lower lip.

"She suggested the same to me. I was planning to bring it up to you tonight too. Thanks, you took the pressure off of me."

"Wait, so you're okay with it?" I asked.

"Well, sure. You've been seeing her on your own, and I've been seeing her on my own. It seems like the next step." Mick shrugged his shoulders as we moved between the hospital, bookstore, and library area. We paused in front of the bookstore, where they set up a front window display of multiple cultures with many different books about the different holidays of each.

"Wow, my first thought was that only couples who had problems had to do couples therapy," I said.

Mick laughed, "Did you tell her that? Because that was my first thought too. I told her you and I had never been better."

I laughed in relief. "Yes, she told me that that is an even better reason to look at some things–

together—that we've individually struggled with in the past. It will help us move forward toward our future."

"Yep, she has us pegged. Hey, maybe we shouldn't each have to pay her if she's telling us the same things."

"Wouldn't that be nice?" I said, knowing the answer to that. "Maybe kids is something we could discuss there."

"Wow, we are on the same page about a lot of things." He leaned down and kissed me, grabbed my hand, and we walked on toward my favorite part of town.

I always wanted to walk through the art district last because that is where the restaurant I co-owned with Ava, Cast Iron Creations, was. Plus, the arts district had the best, most creative decorations.

Delilah, Ava's fiancé, was Leavensport's resident artist owning the craft store, and art gallery with an art store that she took over after her parents retired from the business. Delilah had done window paintings on every large window in the district, including our restaurant. Ours sported a big snowman with black coal eyes and a long carrot nose, a green beanie hat with a pompom, and a long, red scarf blowing behind his back as he marched forward, holding a snowball in the orange-with-black-polka-dot-mittened hands at the end of his wooden arms. There were swirls of magical white, snowy wind below him, and a Christmas tree festooned with red and white candy canes glimmered in the background of the scene. Delilah's paintings always drew people into them, which also, fortunately, drew them into the restaurant.

As we walked the alley, we saw that every window had equally beautiful paintings. The dance studio's windows featured Nutcracker characters, complete with the snow queen, sugarplum fairies, Clara, the Mouse King, and obviously, the Nutcracker himself.

We ended the tour at the Converge Life and Faith Church at the northwest corner of town. The little cobblestoned church welcomed men and women of any faiths and looked beautiful under a blanket of snow.

"Well, what do you think?" I took my last sip of Betsy's hot chocolate and savored the end where all the melted milk chocolate had gathered with leftover marshmallows.

"I think you could have taken me through a junkyard, and I'd be equally impressed with the scenery," Mick said, nuzzling my neck with arms around me.

"We're going to get struck by lightning," I said, looking around the church property.

"What? I'm sure God is okay with me kissing my girlfriend on church grounds." He laughed a sexy deep laugh.

"Jolie!!!!" someone shrieked.

Mick and I turned around to see Mirabelle with her mom walking along with Carlos. Carlos was the assistant manager of our restaurant and was working on opening his own Mexican restaurant this coming spring.

"Hi, guys, what's going on?" I said, cheerfully embracing our hostess with the mostess, as Aunt Fern liked to call her. Mirabelle, a twenty-something woman with Down Syndrome, had the best personality of any person I'd ever met in my life. Her mother, Mary, was a saint in my eyes. I was surprised, though, to see Carlos with them.

"Hello, Miss Jolie," Carlos tipped his tweed flat cap.

"Hi Carlos," I said. Mick reached out to shake his hand, then turned, and he and Mirabelle exchanged a vigorous hug.

"How's Stewart and Lucky?" Mirabelle inquired about Mick's two cats.

"They just told me today how much they miss seeing you," Mick said.

"Really?" She blushed, looking from Carlos to Mary.

Very interesting!

Mary looked at Carlos, who laughed and said, "We will have to plan a date with kitties, Mirabelle."

"Jolie, can I talk to you?" Mary said, grabbing my elbow to move me off to the side while Mirabelle, Carlos, and Mick continued to discuss all things kitties.

"Sure," I said, looking back at Carlos. "What's up?"

"Carlos and I have been seeing each other for some time now," she said, taking note of my surprised look. "I know, I'm sorry we kept it from you. It's just Mirabelle. She hasn't ever met her dad, and I've never dated anyone since him. Also, I'm older than Carlos. But after a few months of dating, we told her and wanted the three of us to work it out before making it known to the entire village."

"Good thinking, and you know if you had told the wrong person, it would take less than five minutes for everyone to find out."

"Exactly," she looked relieved.

"You don't owe me any kind of explanation, Mary—or anyone, for that matter."

"Well, we can't keep it a secret anymore," she said, pointing to her belly.

Oh, I see now.

About the Author

Moving into her second decade working in education, Jodi Rath has decided to begin a life of crime in her The Cast Iron Skillet Mystery Series. Her passion for both mysteries and education led her to combine the two to create her own business, called MYS ED, where she splits her time between working as an adjunct for Ohio teachers and creating mischief in her fictional writing. She currently resides in a small, cozy village in Ohio with her husband and her nine cats.

Other Books by this Author
Book One: *Pineapple Upside Down Murder*
Short Story 1.5 "**Sweet Retreat**"
Book Two: *Jalapeño Cheddar Cornbread Murder*
Book 2.5 A Holiday Book *Turkey Basted to Death*
Book 3 *Blueberry Cobbler Blackmail*

Links So We Can Stay Connected
Be sure to sign up for a monthly newsletter to get MORE of the Leavensport gang with free flash fiction, short stories, two-minute mysteries, cast-iron recipes, tips, and more. Subscribe to our monthly newsletter for a FREE Mystery A Month at http://eepurl.com/dIfXdb

Follow me on Facebook at https://www.facebook.com/authorjodirath

@jodirath is where you can find me on Twitter

www.jodirath.com

Upcoming Releases

Coming December 18, 2020, ***Yuletide Cast of the Iron Skillet***

Coming April 16, 2021, ***Monkey Bread Business***

Coming July 23, 2021, ***Pork Chopped to Death***

Coming October 29, 2021, ***Punkin Strudel Mayhem***

Lightning Source UK Ltd.
Milton Keynes UK
UKHW040646150920
369944UK00001B/389